POISON, PEARLS & PARK AVENUE

PENELOPE BANKS MURDER MYSTERIES

COLETTE CLARK

DESCRIPTION

A murder at a young ladies' luncheon...and no shortage of suspects.

1925 New York

Penelope "Pen" Banks and Constance Gilmore have a notoriously sordid history. Thus, when Constance dies from poisoning at a luncheon for the Young Ladies Historical Preservation Society, Penelope becomes the prime suspect.

In order to clear her name, Penelope must wade through the dirt of New York's most elite families, all of whom have nothing on the gangsters and card sharks she once consorted with when it comes to being unscrupulous.

Along New York City's most famous avenue, secrets, lies, and scandals battle with political ambitions in Penelope's determination to find the true murderer before she finds herself accused of the crime.

***Pearls, Poison & Park Avenue* is the third book in the Penelope Banks Mystery series set in 1920s New York. The enjoyment of a cozy**

historical mystery combined with the excitement and daring of New York during Prohibition and the Jazz Age.

ABOUT THE AUTHOR

Colette Clark lives in New York and has always enjoyed learning more about the history of her amazing city. She decided to combine that curiosity and love of learning with her addiction to reading and watching mysteries. Her first series, **Penelope Banks Murder Mysteries** is the result of those passions. When she's not writing she can be found doing Sudoku puzzles, drawing, eating tacos, visiting museums dedicated to unusual/weird/wacky things, and, of course, reading mysteries by other great authors.

Join my Newsletter to receive news about New Releases and Sales!
https://dashboard.mailerlite.com/forms/148684/72678356487767318/share

CHAPTER ONE

"And...I've caught you!"

Penelope "Pen" Banks's hand fisted, taking hold of the culprit that had caused so much trouble. Not only was the fate of a maid hanging by a thread, but her own reputation as a female private investigator.

There was also the matter of her own wasted time.

"Voila!" She pulled the emerald earring from beneath the couch and lifted it into the air.

A small round of applause rewarded her effort. Penelope rose from the floor and walked it over to Mrs. Winthorpe to drop it into her outstretched hand.

"Miss Banks, you really are the genius your cousin said you were," Mrs. Winthorpe lauded. She turned to offer an encouraging smile to Mrs. Randolph and Mrs. Mortimer on either side of her. The two women obediently offered smiles of appreciation.

Penelope wouldn't have used the word "genius" but she did have a rather unique ability to remember the things she saw as though they were in a photograph. It certainly came in handy in her new profession. Not that she had needed to use it much for this case.

"Well, when you mentioned having removed your earrings while you were reading a magazine on the couch, I thought perhaps the missing one might have fallen beneath it. Odd that the maid didn't think to look there."

The sardonic tone of her voice was seemingly lost on Mrs. Winthorpe. "It *is* so difficult to find good help these days. Though I suppose she will at least be relieved that I no longer suspect her as a thief."

"I'm sure." Again Penelope's tone fell on deaf ears.

"While I have you, Miss Banks," Penelope didn't like the sound of that one bit, "why don't you join us for lunch? Your dear cousin has already agreed to stay."

Penelope cast a quick, exasperated look toward her Cousin Cordelia. She should have known something sinister was afoot when she was invited to handle a "case" for Mrs. Winthorpe. Not only had it been far too easy to solve, but she was the sort of snob who would have never availed herself of something as tawdry as a private detective; not when she could just fire a maid and buy a new pair of earrings.

Which meant she wanted something.

Penelope had spent three years as a social pariah among the elite of New York for reasons she refused to dwell on right now. The rumors that she had made most of her income by illegally playing cards in nightclubs during those three years were quite true. There were still many who believed that the large amount she had been left by her late mother's dearly departed friend, Agnes Sterling, was not enough to sanitize her reputation.

One of those people was standing in front of her right now. She stood between two others who felt the same, at least they did if they wanted to remain in Mrs. Winthorpe's good graces.

"Oh how I wish I *could* join you for lunch, but I have business to attend to."

"Surely your business can hold? After all, one does need to eat."

"I usually get a boxed lunch and take it back to my office."

That had the desired effect of leaving Mrs. Winthorpe and the other matrons perfectly aghast. Pen wasn't sure what scandalized them most, the boxed lunch, the idea of working in an office, or that she had a career at all.

"This is rather important, Penelope," Cousin Cordelia urged.

Penelope sighed. She loved her cousin dearly. When Pen's father had cast her out, Cordelia, his first cousin, had graciously taken her in, to her own detriment. For that Penelope owed her a debt of gratitude.

She cast a shrewd look toward Mrs. Winthorpe. "Perhaps you can simply tell me what it is you plan on asking of me over lunch. I think that would save a lot of unnecessarily wasted time, don't you?"

Mrs. Winthorpe's mouth tightened with displeasure. The other women, Cousin Cordelia included, cast a wary look her way, mostly to take their cues from her reaction.

"Very well, seeing as you have *business* to attend to," she finally conceded, quite unhappily. "I've taken the liberty of including you on the attendee list for the next meeting of the Young Ladies Historical Preservation Society. It's to be a luncheon."

Penelope would have rather died.

"That *was* quite the liberty."

Mrs. Winthorpe smiled with satisfaction, completely

misreading her response. "I knew you would appreciate it. After all, you are one of the prominent young residents of our fair city, a city which we would all very much like to keep fair, no? I have no doubt that an invitation to join the Society will be forthcoming by the end of that luncheon."

Yes, it was *the* society to be a member of if you were a young woman of a certain standing. Most of these societies, organizations, and other banal pastimes the idle, rich female population filled their days with were just that, pastimes. The Young Ladies Historical Preservation Society did have a small degree of power. They put in the work of determining which buildings in New York were deemed "historic" and thus should be preserved for posterity. One word from them passed to the Board of Aldermen and a proposed project could be dead before it started. In this era of constant new development, the Society could have even the most determined developer trembling with worry.

Naturally, membership was by invite only.

"I'm afraid I have to decline," she said, then added just for her own amusement, "I'm far too busy with my job."

Mrs. Winthorpe glared at her. "How disappointing, particularly after your dear cousin *assured* me that you would be amenable, enthusiastic even."

"Did she?" Pen turned her attention to her cousin.

"Well...I—I don't think I—"

"She did," Mrs. Winthorpe insisted, casting a defiant look toward Cousin Cordelia, who cowed under her steely gaze.

Penelope felt her blood turn hot. Though she had to give Mrs. Winthorpe some credit, she knew exactly where to apply the pressure. Penelope didn't give one fig about her own reputation. But she knew how important it was to Cousin Cordelia to be accepted by women like this.

"Well, I suppose I should make an appearance, seeing as I'm so *enthusiastic* about it," Penelope said curtly. "I assume there is some effort they are working toward that requires a large cash donation from the members?"

Mrs. Winthorpe chose to ignore her tone, which was now impossible to miss. Her mouth was now set into a satisfied smile.

"This year's proposed project will be named at the next meeting, and I'm quite sure it will be a very important one. A monument that will surely leave its mark upon the landscape of New York for decades, if not centuries. Just think, Miss Banks, you will be a part of maintaining New York history."

"How grand."

"So you'll attend." It was a statement, not a question.

"How could I refuse?"

"Splendid." Mrs. Winthorpe sounded more smug than pleased. She was a woman who enjoyed getting her way.

"Now, if you'll excuse me, I really do have business to attend to."

Namely, plotting how to extract herself from this invitation without negatively affecting her cousin—with whom she'd have a very long talk later.

CHAPTER TWO

"So you are going after all." Cousin Cordelia breathed a sigh of relief when Penelope entered the living room later that week dressed in something more appropriate for a ladies' luncheon than her standard office attire.

Pen was wearing a soft pink dress with a handkerchief skirt. The long-sleeved overdress was sheer chiffon patterned with flowers. It was paired with a matching pink and white cap with a floral accent. She had to admit, it was rather enjoyable to have a reason to wear one of her nicer day dresses.

Not that she planned on letting her cousin off the hook so easily.

"I don't know why, I abhor the idea of being coerced into these things," Penelope said, briefly narrowing her eyes at her cousin.

The recently adopted Lady Dinah, or "Lady Di," as Cousin Cordelia had taken to calling her, sat on her cousin's lap, purring blissfully away as her new owner stroked her long white fur. Lady's three kittens occupied themselves by going to war with the curtain fringe next to them. Pen remained standing at a distance, hoping they wouldn't suddenly take an interest in rubbing against or scratching at her stockinged legs.

"How can you be coerced into something so enviable?" Cousin Cordelia scoffed. "Do you know how many young women would have loved to be invited to that luncheon? Honestly, Penelope, you baffle me sometimes."

"I'd be more than happy to transfer the invitation to one of them. As it stands, I suspect there is more to it than simple money. Considering the membership, they're hardly in need of my donation, which makes me think there is some design in play, and I intend on finding out what it is."

"Oh, Penelope, not everything is a sinister plot. I think these cases you work on have ruined your sense of goodwill, finding evil intention where there is none."

Pen could see there would be no convincing her cousin so she let it go. "All the same, if I'm going to make my debut into decent society for the second time, I might as well look better than everyone else there."

"You *could* simply think of this as an opportunity, a chance to reunite with all your old friends."

"All my old friends abandoned me the moment I no longer had money. And most of those so-called friends won't be in attendance. It's the *Young* Ladies Historical Preservation Society. Have you forgotten that I'm an old maid?"

"Nonsense, you're only twenty-four, hardly an old maid, my dear. There are plenty of young men who would be more than happy to marry you if only you'd...play a bit nicer. What about your friend Benny Davenport? He's handsome and so charming and funny."

Penelope bit back a laugh. Her friend Benjamin

"Benny" Davenport was most certainly not the marrying type, at least not when it came to women.

"At any rate, you look quite lovely, Penelope."

"You have to say that, you're my cousin," Penelope said with a begrudging smile. She still hadn't completely forgiven her cousin for roping her into this nonsense.

Pen turned to their recent maid who seemed to be working out well so far. "What do you think Jenny, do I look stunning enough to make everyone hate me so much that I'll never be invited again?"

"Oh, Penelope," Cousin Cordelia scolded.

"You look lovely Miss Banks, if you're hoping to cause envy, you'll succeed."

"Why thank you, Jenny," she replied, liking their maid even more. "Then I suppose I should be off," she announced with a weary sigh.

Chives, their butler helped her with her light coat and she took the elevator of their 5th Avenue apartment overlooking Central Park down to where her chauffeur Leonard was waiting with the car.

"I wouldn't fire you if you happened to get into an accident on the way there," she said as he opened the door for her. "Nothing serious, of course, but a broken leg or anything that might keep me from attending this luncheon would be greatly appreciated."

He grinned. "That sounds ominous. Not looking forward to this event I take it?"

"I feel like I'm riding off into battle," she said with a sour look as he got in behind the wheel and drove them off.

"Well, if that's your suit of armor, Miss Banks, you've already won the first round."

Penelope laughed. "Just for that, you get something extra for Christmas this year."

He at least had the effect of lifting her mood. Dressing nicely always made Pen feel better, and now that she had the kale to do it she wasn't *completely* opposed to spending far too much on clothes.

She had been honest with Cousin Cordelia about many of her old "friends" not likely being in attendance today. She recalled that membership was limited to unmarried women under twenty-five. After that they were officially ousted and forced to move on to other endeavors, namely raising their families and running their households.

Everything about it was so depressing, not because Penelope was worried about either her marital status or advanced age, but precisely because she had little interest in succumbing to such a life.

It wasn't a long drive to the Peyton Foundation House where the Society held its quarterly luncheons. It was a former mansion that had been built on 4th Avenue south of Grand Central Station generations ago when the thirties was an ideal address to have in New York. The home had long ago been converted into one of those locations that were part museum, part library, and most importantly a place for society ladies to hold charity bazaars, meetings, and lectures.

Or dull luncheons.

"Wish me luck," Penelope said as Leonard opened the door for her.

"If anyone needs it, it ain't you, Miss Banks," he said with a grin. Most wealthy individuals would be appalled at such frank language from their chauffeur, but she and Leonard had been through enough together and understood each other. Besides, his tomcat ways had come in handy in the past, and Penelope's eye was focused on someone else entirely.

Pen twisted her lips but managed a laugh as she continued to the front door. Really, she was probably making too much of this. There were far worse things in the world than lunch with other young ladies.

At a table near the front stood a woman too old to be part of the Young Ladies Historical Preservation Society. She was at least in her forties, but smartly dressed in a black and tan dress, with a very modern hemline up to her calves.

Penelope briefly wondered if perhaps she had dressed too daintily for this event. She suddenly felt rather precious in her chiffon and silk.

Fortunately, next to her stood a much younger woman Penelope did recognize. She was too young to have been part of Pen's set of friends prior to her fall from grace. Her dress was a pretty floral number with willowy short sleeves and a full tulip skirt.

"Hello Alice," Pen greeted.

Alice Todd was the only daughter among four older brothers, all of them working at their family's bank. Pen had been friendly with David, Alice's second youngest brother, though he had wanted something more than that many years ago.

Alice's large blue eyes went wide with surprise and a hesitant smile came to her lips. "Penelope Banks, I thought I saw your name on the list. So you came after all," she said almost breathlessly.

It wasn't exactly the greeting Pen had expected considering she had been specifically invited.

Then again, she knew Alice's family to be far stuffier than the average family of the millionaire classes. Part of the reason Pen had never really been serious about David was that their mother hadn't deemed the Banks family name "old enough" to be a serious consideration for her son.

There was also Pen's mother with no name whatsoever, and worse, her notorious dinners that resembled the salons in France, with a diverse set of characters. That cemented Penelope's relationship with David as nothing more than friendly.

"I'm so sorry," Alice quickly corrected, brushing a strand of willowy blonde hair from her face with embarrassment. She swept it behind one ear which held a pink pearl earring. "It's wonderful to see you again! I *am* glad you came, of course I am."

"Thank you," Penelope said before Alice went completely overboard in making up for her slight. She had always been so sweet and sensitive Pen didn't want to make her feel worse than she already did.

"I'll just put a checkmark next to your name," Alice said brightly, then continued on in a more practiced and formal way. "This is Miss Mabel Colton, the caretaker of the Peyton Foundation House which so graciously allows us to hold our meetings here. She can direct you to where the luncheon will be held."

"This way, Miss Banks," the woman next to her said with a slightly amused look. She must have been quite used to the petty squabbles and forced politeness among this set.

Miss Colton gave her a moment to remove her jacket and hang it in a small closet with the others before leading her to a staircase. "Just follow the stairs up and then to your left. There is punch being served in the open area."

"Thank you, Miss Colton."

"Please, call me Mabel, all the girls do," she stated with a self-effacing smile.

"In which case, I'm Penelope."

"Penelope." Mabel tilted her head slightly before returning to the table at the front with Alice.

Penelope followed her directions, taking a deep breath as she ascended the stairs. She hadn't expected to encounter a familiar face so early on. She should have realized that most of the women here would be the younger sisters of men and women with whom she'd once been friends. Being the oldest—and glaringly unmarried—attendee would certainly make her stand out, especially with her "disgraceful" past.

In the open area to the right, she saw the gathering of young women. Penelope recognized most of the attendees and forced a smile onto her face. Before she could make an entrance her attention was caught by an attendee surreptitiously exiting a set of sliding doors on the other side. When her eyes met Penelope's an impish smile came to her face.

Katherine "Kitty" Andrews, was a face Penelope certainly did recognize as a member of her own set. She was the same age as Pen, and just as unmarried.

"Penelope Banks, fancy seeing you here," Kitty greeted as she approached.

"I could say the same for you. I wouldn't have thought this was something that would interest you. Hardly the kind of fodder the *New York Tattle* would be interested in."

"You'd be surprised," she replied, waggling her eyebrows. "Young ladies of good standing are particularly delicious to the plebeian classes. Why do you think I'm a member?"

Kitty wrote a society column, though it was more of a gossip sheet than anything. She had always been a troublemaker which at least had the benefit of making Penelope feel less out of place here. Her dark red hair was cut into a permed bob done in a flapper style that she liked to shake with a flick of her head, which she did a lot. Her mouth was seemingly permanently set into a smirk as though everything around her was a source of amusement.

Katherine's father was one of the newest of the wealthiest men in New York. His most recent bout of good fortune had come mostly from interests surrounding automobiles.

Kitty boldly took Pen's arm as though they were dear friends and walked her over to the punch station.

"When I saw your name on the list of attendees I knew I had made the right decision to come. Of course, dear *papah* insisted I make an appearance anyway if only to find out which ancient temple this group was keeping from the gallows, as though everyone doesn't already know. Still, it pays to make certain. He likes to keep up on these things and why not use his daughter as the perfect spy? I am so good at it though, aren't I?"

Penelope had never been much interested in reading any of Kitty's pieces. Even though her old friends had stopped sending invitations to parties, Pen didn't enjoy reveling in their public humiliations.

"Your presence here certainly makes it all worthwhile. Are you expecting a murder?" Kitty had a gleeful note to her voice, which carried, causing several of the nearby young ladies to turn and eye them with wary regard.

"Wreaking havoc as usual, I see," Penelope grumbled as she took a cup of punch from a young waiter in a suit. "I think you'd commit murder yourself if only to cause a scandal you could write about."

"*Moi*," Kitty responded in mock horror. "I'm nothing more than a messenger, darling. Observe and report. I don't make the news, I simply convey it."

"Then I should ask the same question of you. Are you expecting a murder?"

"Not literally," she said in a devilishly ambiguous

manner. She jerked her chin toward a young woman nearby. She wore a yellow dress with a dropped waist that seemed to be back in favor this season. "See Marie there? She was expecting to be named chair this year—they get to choose which project to champion each year. She lost by one vote and was *particularly* upset about it. I don't blame her, it was quite the upset. Everyone was certain she was going to win, none more so than herself."

Penelope studied Marie Phillips, who even now had a sour set to her mouth as though just being here was an affront to her pride. She was the fifth-generation descendant of a man who had bought up a significant portion of land in New Jersey when it was dirt cheap. Her father had taken that money and grown it exponentially by putting it into steel. Her mother was a well-known patron of the arts, using the vast sums of money her husband had to establish theaters and museums all over the city.

"But enough about the others. I know why *I* was pressured into attending, but what on earth made you come?"

"Entrapment."

Kitty seemed to find that amusing for some reason, laughing with delight. "I'm sure."

Penelope considered her with narrowed eyes. "What do you know?"

Kitty held off for a moment, enjoying the suspense, then that impish smile returned. "I do know that Marie isn't the only one upset with our current chairlady. Eleanor Winthorpe over there," she tilted her head in the direction of a pretty young woman in a group of others, "also has quite the bone to pick with madame chair."

The last name caused Penelope to study the young woman more intently. She hadn't noticed her on her first scan of the room. Eleanor Winthorpe was the niece of the same Mrs. Winthorpe that had taken the *liberty* of inviting Pen here. The Winthorpes owned a media empire that was on par with William Randolph Hearst, both in print and now in the expanding media of radio and film.

Eleanor was exceptionally pretty with the sort of aloof features and facial expression that made Pen think of the Gibson Girls from decades ago. She wore a dress in a light shade of blue that flattered her pale skin and contrasted with her dark hair. The blue patterned scarf around her neck only seemed to highlight how elegantly long it was. She felt Pen's gaze on her and met it with a fiercely direct look. A small, barely noticeable smile touched the corner of her lips, though the humor didn't touch her eyes.

Penelope suddenly realized she had Eleanor, not her aunt to thank for the invitation, but couldn't fathom why. Something Kitty said struck her and she turned her attention back to her.

"What does the current chair have to do with anything?"

"Well," Kitty looked toward the top of the stairs. "Ah yes, here she comes."

Penelope followed her gaze and nearly dropped the punch in her hand.

Approaching the open area was none other than Constance Gilmore, the very last person on earth Penelope ever hoped to ever see again.

CHAPTER THREE

Constance Gilmore was pretty in an elfin, self-assured way. She was also devious as anything. Her honey-blonde hair was in a shingled bob that was held back from her heart-shaped face with a pink scarf. Penelope was dismayed to see that she too was wearing a dress with a floral pattern in the same pink color as hers, though thankfully the style was different. It cast a slight pink glow against the perfect strand of pearls surrounding her neck. She looked around the room with an air of confidence that claimed everything in sight as hers.

Until her eyes landed on Penelope.

Constance seemed to be just as struck by Penelope's appearance as Pen was by her arrival.

"What...?" It was all that Penelope could utter upon seeing the woman who had played a major role in her downfall three years ago.

That had been when Penelope had discovered her fiancé, Clifford Stokes and Constance in what could only be described as a compromising position; all on the day before Pen's wedding. Pen had of course cancelled the entire thing, despite how influential Clifford's family was. It had been the scandal of the year. The worst part of it was that Pen's own father had sided against her, cutting her off due to the embarrassment of it all, and leaving her to fend for herself.

In retrospect, perhaps Pen should have been grateful to Constance for exposing Clifford for what he was before she actually married him. Their courtship had lasted only a few months, Penelope being stupidly, blindly in love. Still, she wasn't gullible enough to assume Constance had done it for her benefit.

The fact was, Constance Gilmore simply enjoyed taking things that belonged to others.

Right now she was positively seething. Penelope wondered if she would dare approach her. The two of them hadn't spoken since the infamous incident, which had been hushed up, at least publicly. Constance's family was heavily involved in politics and no one wanted to step on those influential toes. However rumors like that couldn't help but spread, mostly thanks to women like the one standing next to her right now.

Penelope turned to Kitty. "You really are meddlesome."

"I'm not meddlesome, I'm mischievous, there's a distinct difference. And don't blame me for this bit of unpleasantness. As I stated, I'm simply an observer."

"Well, if you're hoping for a scene you won't get one from me. I feel absolutely nothing towards Constance Gilmore, not anymore."

If anything, she wanted a private word with Eleanor, who had most definitely orchestrated this debacle.

"Ah," Kitty said turning her attention back toward the entry. "But do you think Constance feels the same about you?"

Penelope turned back to find Constance still scowling

with resentment. Noting the attention on her from all the other young ladies in the room, she quickly transformed it into a gracious smile.

"Welcome everyone, it's such a pleasure to see all of you again. If you'll excuse me for one moment," she said in a perfectly congenial tone before spinning on her feet and turning to walk out.

Penelope let out a slow breath. She took a sip of her punch to fight the sudden dryness in her mouth.

Her eyes caught Eleanor, who met hers with a level gaze of her own. There was some message there, telling Pen that she absolutely had invited her here by design. The subtle, almost imperceptible shake of her head told her that she had no intention of telling her why, at least not at this moment.

Penelope would get it out of her eventually.

With Kitty standing next to her, now probably wasn't the best time anyway. The savvy reporter would absolutely take note if Pen marched up to Eleanor and demanded an answer. As it stood, Kitty probably didn't even know it was Mrs. Winthorpe who had originally invited Pen.

Penelope understood why Constance had left. Now, all eyes were on her, casting either surreptitious glances or looks of naked curiosity. If she were the kind of woman who felt the need to maintain a facade she would have stood there gallantly taking it. But she was the sort who didn't care and couldn't be bothered.

Penelope set her empty glass down and strode out toward a hallway in the opposite direction. She ended up around a corner where a set of beautiful stained glass doors had been opened to reveal a window with a Juliet balcony that looked down onto the interior courtyard.

Pen wandered over to study them, enjoying the moment she had to herself. She trailed a finger along the design with its swirls and swishes and realized that it was an authentic René Gauthier piece. He was one of the masters of the art nouveau style, at least when it came to stained glass.

The windows of the apartment left to Pen by Agnes had a similar set of doors with his work. They had been a gift from Penelope's mother, Juliette Banks, who had invited him as a guest to one of her infamous dinners. She knew how much Agnes appreciated various types of art and had given them as a gift for her birthday.

The moment of peace was interrupted several minutes later.

"And you said you wouldn't make a scene. You have no idea just how scandalous a dramatic exit can be."

Penelope turned to find Kitty approaching with a grin on her face. She leaned against the side of the window to look at Penelope. "Did you not realize Constance was the chair before you decided to come?"

There was no use denying it had affected her.

"You know I didn't. I have no interest in keeping up with society board members. Luncheons like this are nothing more than a chance for wealthy young women to adjust where their peg is on the social ladder—also something I have no interest in."

"Ah yes, I forgot you're a woman with a career, just like *moi*!"

Penelope shot her a frown. "We're hardly the same."

"Horsefeathers, we're both seekers of the truth, which is often a bit dirty. One of your recent cases certainly had you wading in the muck. You seemed to have no problem having your name in print then."

There was a purpose for that, but Pen was certainly not going to tell Kitty about it.

Instead, she stared out at the garden below. The

window was closed but she could still enjoy the scenery. A young gardener was kneeling among the rose bushes, bent over with his hands in the soil. It was a warm enough spring day that he wore nothing more than a pair of overalls and a sleeveless shirt that showed off well-developed, tan muscles with a glimmering sheen of sweat covering them.

Not a *completely* terrible view.

"Speaking of dirt," Kitty said, a grin coming to her lips as she stared down into a different part of the courtyard.

Penelope followed her gaze and saw that Constance was entering the courtyard. She had pulled a cigarette case out of her bag, a lovely piece inlaid with mother of pearl done in a complicated geometric shape. As she selected a cigarette and brought it to her mouth, she eyed the gardener. She paused, then pulled the cigarette away to say something to him.

He chuckled, his broad back vibrating, then shook his head. It seemed to be more a shake of disbelief than rejection. He turned and said something back to her.

Both Penelope and Kitty leaned in with interest when Constance responded by tilting her head and giving him a kittenish smile. With the window closed, they were too far away to hear the conversation. However, anyone could see that she was flirting with him.

"Well, well, well," Kitty said. "It seems our little Constance found a new toy to play with."

The gardener rose up and pulled his cap from his head. With the back of his hand, he wiped the sweat away from his brow, then brushed the black hair back from his forehead. This gave both onlookers a view of his face, which was quite handsome.

Kitty hummed in appreciation.

He seemed to be of Italian heritage, which made the

scene that much more intriguing. Constance Gilmore had the kind of family—the same as most of the privileged young women here—that would certainly frown upon her even *considering* entertaining the affections of a man of Italian descent, even one born in America. Particularly someone as lowly as a gardener.

He walked over to join Constance. She dug into her purse to pull out a gold lighter and hand it to him. He flicked it and lifted it toward her cigarette, cupping it against the wind so that it almost looked as though he was caressing her face. Considering the way she was eyeing him, he may very well have been.

"I wonder if he's sullied her with some of that dirt on his hands," Kitty muttered.

Penelope couldn't hold back a snort of laughter. Kitty turned to her and waggled her eyebrows, laughing as well.

They turned back to see that the gardener was selecting a cigarette from the case Constance held toward him. He lit it with her gold lighter, then handed it back to her, and she put it back into her purse. The two of them continued to smoke and stare at each other in a way that made it quite obvious they not only enjoyed one another's company but this might not have been their first *tête-à-tête*.

"I wonder what John would have to say about this." At Penelope's questioning look Kitty explained with a smirk. "Constance's fiancé."

Penelope's brow rose and her eyes fell back down to the scene below, considering it in a new light. Now that she was paying attention she could see the engagement ring on the finger of the hand that held onto the cigarette. To Pen, it seemed as though Constance was deliberately showing it off just for the added amusement it offered to the picture.

Then again, she was biased.

They heard the chatter rising back in the open area from which they had escaped. The sound of men's voices reached them and drew their attention away from the scene outside.

"It seems our surprise guest speakers have arrived," Kitty said in a wry voice. She raised one eyebrow and slid her eyes to Pen. "The Dukes, Samuel...and *John*."

"*John Duke* is Constance's fiancé?" Penelope certainly didn't keep up with the society pages, having little to no interest in who was getting married to whom. However, she did know the Dukes. Everyone knew the Dukes. They were akin to the Astors and Vanderbilts, having built their fortune in railways. In fact, anything that ran on a rail line from trains to trolleys and even several of the subways, they most likely either owned or made money from it.

Penelope instinctively turned to look down at Constance again, only to find both her and the gardener gone. She could only surmise where they had escaped to, and for what purpose—none of it painting Constance in a good light.

Still, with nothing more to see below, Penelope wandered back to the open area, Kitty following once again.

Both Samuel and John stood near the entrance looking very important—and as though they'd rather be anywhere else but there. The older Duke wore an expression that seemed to perfectly reflect his impatience at having to indulge the attentions of young women for the next hour. John seemed to be put off by the fact that Constance wasn't there to greet him. As he looked around the room, he became more and more agitated.

"Surely the Dukes don't need the help of this organization to protect a building?" Penelope whispered to Kitty.

"You'd be surprised at how nasty things can get in this town when it comes to progress. Even old money can't win out over new ambition. Still, nepotism is a wonderful thing, no? I wonder which of their illustrious buildings has been the target of a development campaign lately. I would put my money on the Park Avenue House, eyesore that it is."

The Duke House on the southernmost part of Park Avenue was a stately relic of the Gilded Age of New York City when tycoons, barons, and scions were marking their territory in the best neighborhoods of a rapidly developing city. The Dukes no longer lived in the large home, having some time ago relocated further north to more impressive accommodations closer to Central Park.

"It's not so terrible."

"No, but it is wasted space. They live up in the snobby eighties these days. I've heard they intend on turning the Duke House into a private club, which is bound to raise the ire of a few developers. Apparently, Park Avenue is *the* address to have these days. Anyone building one of these new luxury apartment buildings going up everywhere is sure to make a mint. Even all the way down in the thirties."

"Eventually they'll have to let it go, won't they? It will look so out of place, surrounded by so many taller buildings. I read that Marjorie Post Hutton is moving her entire mansion to the penthouse floor of a fourteen-story building somewhere up near 91st. That's over fifty rooms. After she makes her move everyone will want the penthouse level."

"Banana oil, the servants have always lived in the quarters on the top floor," Kitty said with a look of distaste. "And for good reason, it gets so miserable in summer and winter."

"I'm sure the wealthy will find a way to make it comfortable. Besides, I can see the appeal. She'll be away from the noise of the street and have a gorgeous view of the park. I might even consider moving into one someday."

Kitty shrugged and turned her attention back to the Dukes. Alice had come in behind them and seemed to sense their discomfort. She hurriedly led them on into the dining room, pushing open one of the closed sliding doors just enough to let them through and guide them inside. After a few minutes, she came back out, leaving them alone inside.

Eventually, Constance reappeared, with absolutely no hint of soil sullying her porcelain complexion.

"Ladies," Alice announced, taking her cue from the chair's reappearance. With her hesitant, gentle voice it barely rose above the sound of chatter.

Behind her, Mabel entered the open area from the dining room, fully pushing open the sliding doors. She made her announcement in a more reaching voice, "Ladies, if you'll please enter and be seated for lunch."

Kitty and Penelope waited for most of the others to go first. Eleanor and her friends were among the first to enter the room. As the crowd thinned out, Penelope noted that Constance seemed to be making a point of being the last to enter. Pen had no desire to be left alone with her old enemy so she followed the last group to head inside. Kitty came with her.

Constance was indeed the last to enter, heading up to the short stage to greet her fiancé who stood there with his father.

"*Darling*, you made it," she said, greeting him with a perfectly innocent smile.

"Of course, you insisted," he said in a terse voice, returning a tight smile.

His forced smile disappeared as soon as she turned to greet his father. He seemed to make a point of not looking out toward the room. Perhaps he was uncomfortable being on stage. When Constance turned around to face the room, he leaned over to whisper something to his father, who nodded in agreement.

Penelope looked around, hoping to find an empty seat as far away from Constance and the raised stage with her fiancé as possible. A frown came to her face when she noted the small white cards at each setting.

"Place cards," Kitty whispered with wicked delight in her voice.

Pen's frown deepened when she realized the only three empty seats left were at a table near the front. Her dreaded assumption was confirmed when Kitty grabbed her arm and led them that way.

Already seated at the table were Alice, Marie, and Eleanor. The two seats on one side of the table right next to each other were Kitty's and hers. The third, directly across from Pen was the last empty chair, obviously reserved for Constance.

This was no mere coincidence.

Penelope turned to Kitty with a glare. "Mischievous is most definitely the correct word."

CHAPTER FOUR

KITTY WORE AN EXPRESSION OF ABSOLUTE INNOCENCE as she took the seat next to Penelope where her place card was.

This explained why Pen had caught her sneakily exiting the dining room when she first arrived. She had most definitely reorganized where each place card was so that the current occupants were seated at this table. Or at the very least, so that she and Penelope were sitting across from Constance.

There was little to be done about seating arrangements now that all the other attendees had taken their seats. Penelope could hardly make a scene by asking to switch with one of the other young ladies, which would only put them both on the spot.

Penelope wasn't the only one upset with the seating arrangement.

Marie looked as though she was going to be sick over it. Her brow was furrowed in consternation as she frowned down at the empty place before her, already imagining having to sit on Constance's left for the hour-long lunch that was to come.

Eleanor, on Constance's right, maintained a perfectly impassive expression. She casually sipped the punch that had already been poured ahead of time. But Penelope could see how white the fingertips of her right hand were as she firmly gripped the glass.

Next to Penelope, sitting on Eleanor's right, Alice's brow wrinkled in confusion, as though this certainly hadn't been where she expected to be seated. Having no doubt been coerced into helping set up this event she would have known where everyone was originally supposed to be seated.

On stage, Constance didn't seem to take note of it as she looked out onto the room to get everyone's attention and make her introductions.

"Ladies, welcome to the first official quarterly meeting for the Young Ladies Historical Preservation Society of 1925. As your elected chair—" she cast a quick, smug smile toward Marie, who was still staring hard at the table "—it is my duty to choose a New York landmark for us to rally around and protect from the dangers of a little *too* much progress. I don't need to remind you that these buildings we select are what have made our great and wonderful city what it is. This is particularly true in an age where it seems as though the modern world is moving at such a fast pace all around us. Everywhere you look people are raging onward into the future, transforming our city into something...different. New faces from all over the world arrive at our borders, clamoring to leave their imprint on our culture and heritage. And while there is nothing inherently wrong with that—"

Penelope had to strain from rolling her eyes. Not a

single person in the room could misunderstand the political meaning behind those words.

"—we ladies of society know the importance of never forgetting who and what made this country what it is. We mustn't forget our past."

Pen had to silently laugh at the irony of that statement from Constance of all people. She wondered if Constance had forgotten her own past with Clifford Stokes.

"It was, of course, a difficult decision choosing only one building to preserve for posterity. New York is a city so ripe with magnificent structures that reflect its rich beginnings, and continued importance on the world stage. However, as chair, I have finally settled on one, a building that reminds us of an era when growth in this city meant something beautiful and momentous. This year's structure is..." she paused for effect, "the Duke House on Park Avenue."

There was another pause. It took a moment for the room to realize that she expected them to applaud her decision. John Duke was the first to do so, coughing with embarrassment before he did. That led everyone else to do the same. The only holdouts were the senior Duke, who seemed to find it beneath him, Marie, who still refused to look up from the table, and Penelope, who refused out of spite.

Kitty cast a wry grin her way as though to say, "I told you so."

Yes, nepotism was a very convenient thing for those who could benefit from it. Penelope thought it rather shameless of the Dukes to make an appearance just to bask in their triumph, though perhaps this was how it was done?

"Today, we are lucky to have the patriarch of the Duke family, and my future father-in-law—" Constance turned to offer a pretty smile toward Samuel "—here to talk more about the history of this beautiful testament to the Gilded Age of New York."

She was the one to lead the round of applause this time. It was cut short by Samuel standing up and shooting a stern look around the room.

"Thank you, Miss Gilmore."

Penelope sipped her punch as he droned on about rail lines and how important they were. Yes, yes, the Dukes' business had left its imprint on this city and a good part of the country since before the Civil War, which made them officially "old" New York. It was quite tiresome to be reminded of these things. Thankfully, he wasn't the long-winded sort—or perhaps he simply wanted nothing more than to be gone. When he was done, he needed no prompting for the round of applause, which had a note of relief in it. He wasn't the most entertaining speaker.

"Alright ladies, this is where the real work begins," Constance said as she retook the podium. "As members of the Young Ladies Historical Preservation Society, it behooves us to put in the effort to actually *preserve*. Alice Todd has graciously offered to come up with a plan of action and assign duties to our members to carry out. But for now, let us enjoy lunch."

Alice, sitting next to Pen, exhaled and looked overwhelmed at the prospect.

"One would think that it should be left to the chairlady to do the work of coming up with a plan of action don't you think?" Kitty asked from Penelope's other side, staring directly at Alice.

Alice quickly blinked and forced a smile to her face. "Oh, I don't mind."

"That's awfully generous. It seems you'll be the one,

ahem, *constructing* a plan of action," Kitty said with an ambiguous smile as she took her glass of punch to drink.

Penelope noticed what effect that statement had on Alice, who swallowed hard and picked up her glass to drink rather than comment further.

"Oh for pity's sake, Kitty, leave Alice alone about that. Heaven knows she has enough on her plate with Constance," Marie scolded.

On stage, Constance was making her goodbyes to her fiancé and his father, who apparently weren't staying to enjoy the lunch. Once they had exited, she turned her attention to the table and a scowl finally appeared on her face.

"Well, this is certainly an interesting arrangement," Constance said in a terse voice when she finally came to join them. She cast a quick hard, accusatory look Alice's way.

Before the poor thing could argue her defense, Constance had moved on to a new victim.

"Katherine, I'm glad to see you received the memo about the new dress code. Trousers, pants, slacks, and breeches have no place among young ladies. The only one you're embarrassing is yourself."

"In my defense, I *had* planned on going golfing right after the last meeting. I do so enjoy going a round or two," Kitty said with a sly look.

Constance didn't so much as twitch a smile, though a few others did. Even the seemingly unflappable Eleanor seemed dryly amused.

"However," Kitty said, waving a hand in the air and smiling pertly, "in the future, I shall make sure to schedule my day accordingly. No more golf interfering with your plans. Perhaps we should compare schedules so it doesn't get awkward?"

Something simmered in the air between them, Constance glaring and Kitty smiling smugly. Penelope had the feeling she had stumbled into something that had already started. It felt like opening a book on chapter twenty and having no idea how the scene she'd landed on had even begun.

The chicken was being served by a team of waiters coming in through a side door. The dish of chicken, potatoes, and green beans with onions was as lackluster as Penelope expected. She quietly wondered if it would cause a minor fuss if she left early.

"What is this?" Marie cried out as her plate was set before her. "I see onions. I specifically asked ahead of time not to include them on my plate. Take it away and bring me what I requested!"

The attention of everyone at the table was arrested by her outburst. Apparently, having to sit next to Constance was taking its toll on her nerves.

"My apologies, ma'am. I'll take it right back and have it made to your *exacting* standards." That came out as impertinent as the waiter had intended. Penelope wondered how much he wanted to be fired that day because Marie looked as though she was on the warpath.

"I beg your pardon?" Marie snapped, shooting him a hard glare.

"Just obeying the lady's wishes," he said, his brow mockingly raised in a questioning manner.

Marie waved her hand across the table, nearly knocking over her punch and that of both people on either side of her, Constance and Kitty. "Take it away and be grateful I'm in no mood to report you to your superiors."

There was something hard in his eyes as he wordlessly took the plate back and walked off. Pen doubted it would come out again, and if it did it would probably be cold or interfered with in a way that was far worse than unwanted onions.

"My, my Marie, you should stick to pink, that color suits you better than tyranny," Kitty said with a laugh.

"And subtlety was never *your* color," Marie snapped back.

"Marie, you *are* looking a bit green. Is there something....weighing on you?" Constance asked.

Penelope blinked in surprise. Was Constance actually showing an ounce of sympathy? But then, her expression was too overly concerned to be anything but an act. Green was obviously a reference to envy rather than any ailment.

Marie glowered at Constance, though her face did go a bit pale as she gritted out, "I'm fine."

Kitty was quick to interject her own mischief onto someone else. "Eleanor, what do you think of this year's official rescue from the firing squad? Have you ever visited the Duke House?"

If Eleanor was affected by some underlying assault, she didn't show it. She assessed Kitty with cool eyes. "Of course I have, as you well know. Still, I consider this year's choice to be unwise. I think it a rather *uninteresting* relic of the *past*."

That seemed to have some intended meaning, and Penelope eyed Eleanor and Constance sitting next to one another. Now that she had a better look, she could see that the scarf Eleanor wore around her neck looked quite similar to the one Constance had holding back her hair, except in pink instead of blue.

"Marie is right, for once," Constance said. "Subtlety

isn't your color, Kitty. Perhaps you should occupy your mouth with the lunch being served instead. After all, we wouldn't want you to have to take back anything you've said, would we?"

That somehow had the effect of shutting Kitty up.

Penelope's eyes bounced around the table, wondering what was going on. There seemed to be quite a degree of coded language and subtle insinuations.

"Penelope, I'm rather surprised to see you at the *Young* Ladies Historical Preservation Society." Constance drew her attention, making sure to stress the word, "Young." "You'll be twenty-five soon, no?"

Penelope was quite used to Constance's biting ways and it sailed right off her.

"Not soon enough," she replied cordially.

"And still unmarried it seems," Constance lamented. She quickly brightened back up as she picked up her glass of punch, holding it higher than necessary so that her engagement ring was on display. "But surely you'll be attending *my* wedding. Now that you've been welcomed back into society, I'll make sure you get an invitation. It's to be held in two weeks."

Her eyes had a wicked gleam as she took a long sip of her punch, waiting for Penelope's reaction.

Penelope didn't respond right away, knowing that the entire table was waiting for a quick reflexive barb.

"John Duke," Penelope finally said in a congratulatory tone. "Though, I was surprised to discover it wasn't Clifford Stokes. I know you two were once...an item."

Constance, grimaced, practically snatching her glass away from her lips. The rest of the table went still, staring at the both of them with wide eyes.

Penelope had dared mention his name, and she had enjoyed it so much she continued.

"Still, I'm sure John will appreciate the wealth of, ahem, *experience* you bring to the marriage."

"Oh," Alice squeaked out in shock.

Eleanor finally showed something beyond the barest hint of emotion with a bold laugh. She grabbed her punch and lifted it in salute toward Penelope.

Marie was perfectly ashen with shock.

Kitty simply stared at Penelope, her mouth forming an O of gleeful incredulity. Pen could already read the headlines of the next gossip papers.

She should have felt bad about it, but she simply couldn't muster that much sympathy for Constance. It was obvious that several of the young ladies here had been a victim of her cruelty, selfishness, and vindictiveness. Perhaps this might be a lesson for her.

Constance was apoplectic, so filled with rage she couldn't speak. She slammed her glass down on the table hard enough to cause the punch to splash out onto the tablecloth.

"Constance!" Marie protested as some splatter hit her dress.

"I'm sure she meant that in the nicest way, Constance," Alice cried, staring at her in dismay.

"You've left her speechless, Pen. Congrats on accomplishing *that* feat," Kitty said with a sharp laugh next to her.

"I think...there might be something wrong with her," Alice said, now looking even more concerned.

Constance was still silent, and it had gone long enough for everyone at the table to suspect it wasn't due to rage but something else. When she grabbed her stomach, her face a picture of extreme pain, Alice screamed. Eleanor backed away. Marie stared in horror.

"Something's wrong!" Eleanor shouted.

That caught the attention of everyone in the room.

Constance grabbed her throat, her fingers clawing at it. They hooked into the edge of her necklace and viciously tugged, casting the pearls everywhere.

"Someone call for a doctor!" Kitty shouted.

Penelope was the only one who could see that it was too late.

When Constance pushed back in her chair, then doubled over and fell to the floor, Pen knew for sure. She began writhing, coughing up a bit of blood. That confirmed the suspected cause of what would soon be her death.

"My God, she's been poisoned," Penelope said in a soft voice.

CHAPTER FIVE

Although Penelope's announcement that Constance had been poisoned had been barely audible, it had a ripple effect throughout the room.

Screams filled the air. Glasses of punch were practically thrown back onto tables. Forks and knives clattered against plates. Chairs were pushed away as though the tables themselves were poisonous. One of the waiters dropped his entire tray of chicken dishes.

That was enough to snap Penelope out of her momentary paralysis. She shot up from the chair and rounded the table to kneel next to Constance who had finally gone still. While pandemonium erupted around her, she calmly lifted the head of her former rival and found lifeless blue eyes staring back at her. The pearls scattered around her created a particularly morbid picture. The remainder were still attached and hung loosely from a silver clasp with an engraving of an A on it.

"We need to call the police," she said to the nearest person.

Unfortunately, that person happened to be Alice, who

simply stared down at her like a terrified rabbit. Penelope noted that the pearls in her ears matched the ones now scattered around Constance's body, which had in fact been pink.

Next to Alice, Marie emptied the meager contents of her stomach at the grotesque scene before her. That did nothing to defuse the terror filling the room, which shot up a few degrees, now that everyone assumed more than one glass of punch or plate had been poisoned.

"I'll call them," Kitty said, rushing out.

"Are you sure it's poison?" Eleanor asked.

"Isn't it obvious?" Penelope said looking up at her. Eleanor's eyes seemed filled with horror, perhaps because only moments before she had joined in the pleasure of witnessing Constance's comeuppance.

There would be time for regret later. Right now, Penelope knew they needed to keep everyone in attendance in the room, or at least keep them from escaping in a panic.

"Go and get Miss Colton. She needs to get everyone settled and make sure they don't leave the building."

Eleanor, to her credit, seemed to catch on quickly and gave Penelope a quick nod before rushing out.

"Who would want to kill Constance?" Alice cried.

Penelope didn't bother answering, mostly because she knew that she would be considered number one on that list of people.

Already her mind was working, trying to piece together how the crime had been committed. The only thing Constance had eaten or drank was the punch. So when had the poison been added to her drink? More importantly, by whom?

There were too many suspects to narrow it down, starting with everyone at the table she shared.

"Don't touch anything!" she cautioned in a stern voice.

Alice jumped away from the table as though it was on fire. Marie, seemingly recovered, stood up and took two steps back. She stared down at Constance with a numb look on her face.

"Ladies, ladies," she heard Mabel Colton's voice eventually call out. "I ask that you please calm down. Panicking won't help. The police have been called and are on their way."

"I want to go home!" someone cried out.

"I know, this is a difficult situation. However, I can't allow you to leave until—"

"You can't keep us here!"

"My father will hear about this!"

"Someone in this room is a *murderer*!"

That seemed to set everyone off once again, all the young ladies crying, screaming, protesting, and worse, trying to escape.

"Quiet, everyone!" This was Eleanor, who, despite being almost twenty years younger than Mabel, had ten times the authority based solely on her last name. "As Mabel said, a crime has been committed. No one is allowed to leave until the police arrive. Obviously, we won't require you to stay in this room. I think perhaps the library would be fitting?" She turned to Mabel, who nodded her agreement.

"I don't know why all of us have to stay. It's obvious who killed Constance."

Penelope didn't even need to look up to know that everyone's eyes were suddenly directed her way. She rose up from where she had knelt next to Constance, realizing too late how guilty it made her look having rushed to her side so soon before her death.

"We have no idea what happened," Mabel said in a stern voice. "When the police arrive, they are going to question everyone. I strongly suggest that you not resort to speculation and rumor before then. This is a very serious crime that has been committed."

That did nothing to diffuse the strong stench of guilt that surrounded Penelope. It clung like a scarlet letter, which Pen found particularly ironic, being that she hadn't been the one to cheat once upon a time.

"I think Miss Winthorpe's suggestion we retire to the library is a good idea. Please come along now, ladies."

This time there was no protest. Like scared sheep, they willingly followed Mabel's lead.

When most of them had gone, Mabel turned her attention to the women still near Constance's body.

"I'm afraid that includes all of you as well. It's probably best if this room remains closed off. I'll also need to go and gather the staff." She sighed, looking suddenly worried. "I'm sure the police will want to talk to them as well."

The police would not only want to talk to them, they'd probably focus on them first. In a room filled with the daughters of New York's most prominent families, that much was highly predictable.

Penelope's mind reversed back to what she had witnessed in the courtyard. She knew the gardener would be the first person they set their sights on for a number of reasons. Never mind that one of the attendees was right, Penelope should be their number one suspect.

The Peyton Foundation House was located below midtown, which meant it was outside of the area covered by the 10A precinct, where Detective Richard Prescott worked. Having worked with him before, Penelope knew that he at least was an honest member of law enforcement, unlikely to be swayed by influence or prejudice. She had no idea who the local precinct would send.

Right now, it was upon Penelope to pay close attention to everything and everyone. Her ability to remember what she saw would come in particularly handy for this murder. If only to save some poor, innocent soul who didn't have the benefit of parents that lived on 5th Avenue.

Or perhaps to save herself.

CHAPTER SIX

"I can't believe it," Kitty said. For once, there was no undercurrent of devilish delight at the misfortune of others.

"Can't you?" Penelope said quietly next to her. She was still shaken by the image of Constance's lifeless face.

Still, right now, Pen was more concerned about who may have done it. She wanted to pry information out of her, mostly concerning the barbs shot back and forth at the table just before Constance had died. Unfortunately, they were packed into the library, members of the Young Ladies Historical Preservation Society and staff together. Not only could anyone overhear them, but most people in the room also had their attention studiously glued on Penelope.

She stood by the window, which had the same René Gauthier stained glass doors opened to let in the light through the window. These windows faced 4th Avenue. Penelope consciously avoided catching anyone's eyes. Kitty was the only one who would even come near her.

Alice had finally succumbed to tears and was practically inconsolable. Several of the ladies sat nearby, trying to comfort her.

Marie was aware that most people in the room knew there was no love lost between Constance and her, but her chin stayed defiantly raised.

Eleanor had a circle of friends surrounding her once again and she had reverted to her aloof manner, showing as little emotion as possible.

The group of waiters was huddled in a circle quietly but intensely talking. They were no doubt plotting out how they would defend themselves against the blame that the police would surely lay at their feet. Having served the punch, they would make an easy target. Penelope felt bad for them being lassoed into this trouble. They probably hadn't expected a dead body when they agreed to work this event.

The gardener stood in a corner by himself, looking around uneasily. He was probably wondering if anyone here had seen Constance and him earlier.

Mabel was firmly situated in a chair by the door in case anyone got ideas about leaving before the police arrived. As the de facto captain of this ship, she now had the look of someone who had just experienced a catastrophic storm.

The bell announced the arrival of the police and Mabel quickly stood, breathing out a sigh of relief. As she left to let them in, everyone else in the room seemed to react, the chatter starting once again. Pen could see the indignation come back to the young ladies' faces. She could also see the wary expressions come to those of the staff. The gardener looked perfectly petrified.

Mabel was gone for a while, no doubt showing the police the scene of the crime and explaining what had happened. Penelope hoped she had been sensible enough to keep it strictly to the facts. She eventually came back with the detectives and two police officers in uniform.

"Alright, everyone," the older detective began. He had the cynical, grizzled look of someone who had been at this game for too long, and even this couldn't affect him. "I'm Detective Beaks and this is Detective Reynolds."

The other detective was only slightly younger but he seemed more alert, casting a hard, beady eye at everyone in the room, particularly the staff.

"I understand this is upsetting, but I just have a few questions for most of you, then you'll be on your way."

Before he could begin, there was another ring from the front door. Mabel quickly left to go and answer it.

Penelope saw both detectives cast quick, wary glances at each other. They knew the sound of obstruction about to happen. Sure enough, an older, important-looking man in a suit barged into the library. Either someone else must have used the phone to call their family, or someone at the police station informed said family. It wasn't beyond belief that certain members of the police department might want to curry favor with influential families, or perhaps simply get paid. Either way, word was going to spread like wildfire now.

"I'm here for Miss Parsons. I'm her family attorney," he said, looking around the room, then casting a penetrating gaze at the detectives. "I certainly hope you haven't started questioning her without my counsel."

A young woman instantly popped up from her chair. "Am I free to go, Mr. Gibbons?"

"You most certainly are," he replied, casting another hard look at both detectives. "If you intend on questioning my client, you'll make an appointment and it most certainly won't be outside of my presence."

"We have a list of all attendees," Detective Beaks said casting a quick glance toward Mabel who nodded her head in agreement. "We'll be in touch if we need to speak to Miss Parsons."

"Good," he replied, hurriedly ushering his client out.

"Does that mean the rest of us can leave as well?" another attendee asked.

"We need everyone who was sitting with the deceased—"

"Constance Gilmore," Mabel corrected in a terse voice. "That was her name."

Detective Beaks exhaled softly with exasperation. "Anyone sitting at the table with *Miss Gilmore*, you'll need to stay."

He turned to give Mabel a pointed look. She stared back a moment before realizing what he wanted.

"Ah, yes." She gave an apologetic smile before identifying each of the women who had been seated at the table with Constance.

"Okay, you five stay, the rest of the attendees are free to leave," he said in a brusque voice, addressing the young ladies in the room in a manner they weren't used to.

"And what about us?" One of the waiters demanded as the ladies quickly rose and made their way out of the library. Penelope noted it was the one who had been rude to Marie earlier, as much as it may have been warranted at the time. "We should be able to leave too."

Detective Beaks cast a humorless look his way. "You're going to stay right there."

"I see how it is. The rich get to go on their merry way and we working men have to bow to your mercy."

That unfortunate complaint did nothing but make him a target.

"Bow, sit, stand, I don't care, but you ain't leaving until I say so."

"Don't we have rights too? We had nothing to do with this, and you have no probable cause to hold us."

He was doing a fine job of getting the rest of the waiters worked up. Even the few remaining young women who were once so eager to leave now lingered, waiting to see what explosion he would set off.

The gardener was wise enough to subtly distance himself from them so as not to get caught in the buckshot scatter that was surely coming their way.

"You some kinda Bolshevik?" Detective Reynolds asked, giving him a hard look.

"So that's how it's going to be? You applying labels because you've finally met with someone who knows the law? Who knows their rights? Call me what you like, but the fact remains, I do in fact know my rights. We don't have to stand for this tyranny."

"This ain't Russia, Bolshie. You and your *comrades* will stand there until I tell you you're free to leave. Otherwise, I'll bust you for obstruction."

Penelope could see the train wreck this was heading toward and decided to step in before things got even more out of hand.

"I'm sure that Detective Beaks and Detective Reynolds both understand everyone's rights and have no intention of unnecessarily holding anyone longer than they have to. We all just want to help find out who killed Constance. I'm certain this includes you, Mr...?" Penelope gave the waiter a questioning look.

He stubbornly scowled at the detective for a moment longer before relaxing and turning to Penelope. "No Mister, just Wyatt. Wyatt Clemson."

"Mr. Clemson," she said brightly, then turned to the detectives. "Right, well, I for one am perfectly fine waiting until after you've briefly questioned Mr. Clemson, and the rest of the staff before you make your way to me."

"Me too," Kitty, announced. Penelope was sure she was all too happy to stay if only to gobble up any tasty tidbits that might be dropped for her column. Already, this was proving to be a perfect smorgasbord.

"I'm fine waiting as well," the ever-accommodating Alice said.

The detectives, sensing a consensus in the room, turned their attention to Eleanor.

She stared back, perfectly impassive. "I, on the other hand, would rather dispense with this quickly. I don't like the idea of being in the same room as a possible murderer."

Penelope silently sighed with dismay but wasn't surprised.

"Well, I certainly didn't kill her, and I see no reason why I should have to stay in order to prove that. Isn't there something about innocent until proven guilty?" Marie protested, seemingly recovered from the shock of seeing Constance dead.

"Hear, hear!" Wyatt added, getting worked up again.

"Quiet!" Detective Beaks roared.

When everyone had been stunned into silent attention, he continued.

"No one is under arrest and this isn't an interrogation, but we do need to get the facts and since most of you were with the deceased just prior to death, that makes you important witnesses. Understood?"

Everyone silently nodded.

"Good, Detective Reynolds will start with you," he

nodded toward Marie, "and I'll be questioning you," he nodded toward Eleanor.

A wise decision to get them over with first.

He turned to Wyatt with a wry smile on his face. "You wait right there for your turn."

Blessedly, Wyatt didn't argue.

"From there we'll work our way through everyone else." He seemed to finally note the gardener trying to look invisible in the corner. He turned to Mabel. "Who's this one?"

"Oh, he's just the gardener. I thought everyone in the building at the time should be gathered in the same place, but I hardly think—"

"What's your name?" Detective Beaks interrupted, turning his attention back to the young man and scrutinizing him more closely.

"I, um, it's Sal, sir," he said, straightening up. Now that he had been detected he no longer cowered.

Detective Reynolds cast a narrow-eyed look his way. "What's your last name, *Sal*?"

Sal paused, working his jaw as he returned a sardonic look. "Rizzo."

Both detectives coughed out sharp laughs and gave each other knowing looks. "We'll get to you eventually—*Sal* is it? That your real first name?"

Sal's chin lifted and a dark look came to his eyes. "Salvatore Rizzo," he said defiantly, almost as though declaring war.

Penelope admired it, even if it did him absolutely no favors.

"Just as I suspected," Detective Reynolds muttered with a sneer.

The detectives gestured for Marie and Eleanor to follow them, then turned to the two policemen who had come with them. Without saying a word they knew it was their duty to keep watch and make sure no one left the room.

Salvatore seemed to deflate once they were gone, sagging back against the wall. He twisted his lips as he turned to angrily stare out the window at the street. His hand dropped into one of his pockets and he pulled out a pack of cigarettes. After sticking one in his mouth, he put the pack back and dug around for a lighter or box of matches.

Instead of pulling anything out, he blinked hard and his gaze sharpened in alarm. He quickly snatched the cigarette from his mouth and stared at it, as though wondering what to do with it.

"*Salvatore*," Mabel snapped. "You know better than to smoke in the library."

"Yeah sorry, Mabel—I mean Miss Colton." He crumpled it in his hand, which seemed a perfect waste to Penelope. He looked around uneasily as though wondering where to put the remains.

Pen quickly looked away before he noticed her watching, but noted him in her periphery.

He casually wandered to a small trash can and dumped the cigarette remains there. With both hands stuffed into his pockets, he continued to wander, strolling about looking at the books on the shelves. Penelope could understand why he'd be nervous; the detectives already showed their prejudice. He finally plopped down onto one of the overstuffed couches and seemed to relax.

Penelope turned her attention to the waiters who were once again huddled in the corner, animatedly talking amongst themselves. There seemed to be some debate going on, and Wyatt, as the designated ringleader was the most lively of them all, angrily stabbing the air with his finger.

He was quite obviously a communist, or perhaps one of those anarchists. Some kind of -ist at any rate. Penelope had nothing against any of them, it was what made this city interesting, but it certainly hadn't been smart to reveal so much to the police when a murder charge was on the line. Now they seemed to be plotting some kind of uprising, which would only complicate things.

Penelope wasn't the only one watching them. Kitty studied them with a hint of a smile, knowing trouble was about to erupt. Mabel had a firm set to her mouth, words of admonishment already forming on her tongue to stop them before they started. Alice, no longer crying, stared with eyes widened in fright. Even Salvatore seemed amusedly interested in what they might be planning, no longer worried that he might be tainted by association.

When Wyatt finally broke from the group, a determined look on his face Penelope could feel a sizzle of electricity in the room.

"*Don't!*" Alice squeaked out, surprising everyone, even herself. She blinked and violently colored with embarrassment when she realized all eyes were now on her.

"I just...it isn't worth it, is it?" she pleaded.

He stared at her, still as inflamed as a bull facing a matador. The policemen were standing at attention, ready to get physical if need be.

"I suggest you listen to the young lady, bub," one officer said.

Penelope was set to intervene yet again when the two detectives came back. They could sense trouble in the air and their focus rightfully fell on Wyatt.

"What have we got here now?"

"Just wondering how long you're going to continue to detain us," Wyatt said, arms crossed over his chest.

"Not to worry, you're next up, Marx," Detective Reynolds said with a dark smile. "In fact, the lot of you come with me."

"And you," Detective Beaks said, staring hard at Salvatore. "You're all mine."

Salvatore's jaw tightened with anger and a sullen look came to his eyes, but he rose from the couch. His earlier trepidation was gone, now replaced with a confident swagger that showed no hint of concern.

Penelope wondered what had changed. Perhaps he was just putting on a facade, knowing that showing fear would only make him look guilty. Still, the taunting smirk he sported indicated something more.

In her head, Pen replayed everything she'd seen of him while they were sequestered here. With eyes slowly narrowed, she realized what had happened to make him so confident.

CHAPTER SEVEN

Penelope knew better than to immediately make any moves to confirm her suspicions about Salvatore. Not only would the two police officers notice her, but Kitty would become curious. Hopefully, the detectives would take advantage of her willingness to be interviewed last.

"So who do you think did it?" Kitty asked.

"How could I possibly know?" Penelope replied with a tired sigh.

"You're the detective, no? I thought that's what you did?"

"Detect? Yes, that is what I do, not jump to conclusions." Penelope turned to her with a shrewd look. "Speaking of which, you're the one with all of the, as you called it, dirt. What was going on at the table during lunch?"

Kitty's eyes went wide with innocence. "Whatever do you mean?"

"Playing coy doesn't suit you, Katherine Andrews. It was obvious that both you and Constance were holding information about the others, as well as each other. And it certainly doesn't take a detective to know that it was you who changed the place cards so we would all be at the same table."

Kitty stared at her for a moment, her expression blank before succumbing to a small, abrupt laugh. This earned her scolding looks from both Alice and Mabel. The two police officers also took more notice of them.

"Okay, you've found me out. Yes, I changed the place cards. How was I to know one of them would kill her?"

"You assume it was one of them?"

"Who else could it be?" Kitty said, a look of confusion on her face, it brightened again. "Was it you?"

"No, for heaven's sake."

"Does this mean you'll be taking this case? Who would have figured, Penelope Banks, solving the murder of the girl who once—"

"This isn't my case to take on," Penelope interrupted. "I don't make it a habit of interfering with police investigations."

Not *entirely* true. There was one detective in particular who could attest to the fact that Penelope Banks was quite meddlesome when it came to police investigations. Still, Kitty didn't need to know that.

"You do realize you'll be a primary suspect. I'd be willing to bet both Marie and Eleanor are pointing the finger at you as we speak."

"Thanks to the person who sat me at the table with Constance in the first place," Penelope accused.

Kitty shrugged. "I'm happy to tell them you were well on the other side of the table out of reach of her glass."

"How ever can I thank you?" Penelope retorted.

Kitty laughed at the sarcasm in Pen's voice, once again earning them both looks of disapproval. "Give me an exclusive for your next big case and I'll tell you everything."

"If you think I'll have anything to do with you after today, then—"

Penelope was interrupted by the return of Detective Beaks, who had apparently finished with Salvatore. Detective Reynolds was no doubt still enjoying twisting the screws with the "Bolshevik" wait staff.

That was quick, Penelope thought to herself.

Noting how agitated Alice was, sitting by herself wringing her hands, he wisely chose her next before she completely disintegrated.

When they were gone, Kitty turned back to Penelope with a pout. "Don't be like that, Pen. I'd hate to think I've ruined our friendship over one silly bit of fun."

"Silly? Fun? And what friendship? I don't recall you ever once calling on me after I moved from 5th Avenue to 35th Street."

"Well, if you're going to hold that against me—"

Detective Beaks came back, interrupting Kitty.

This was all going much faster than Penelope would have predicted. Perhaps her fear that they would happily and easily lay the blame on a member of the staff was unwarranted.

"I suppose I'll go next," Kitty said, giving Penelope another pout as she walked over to the detective.

That left only Mabel and the policemen with Penelope. None of them seemed interested in her, being that she hadn't yet caused any fuss. She used the moment to stare out the window and think, replaying the day's events in her head.

Constance wasn't the most likable person, and that was putting it mildly. Marie was upset about losing the chair position, but that was hardly a murderous offense, was it? There was definitely some venom in Eleanor, who had a reason for inviting Penelope in the first place, though she was still clueless as to why. Alice had been turned into Constance's worker bee, but Penelope wasn't sure if that was due to blackmail or simply the ease with which the poor girl allowed herself to be used.

Though, there were the pearls to consider.

The ones around Constance's neck had been identical to those on Alice's ears. The silver clasp confirmed they were indeed Alice's. Penelope recognized them from a brief glimpse she'd had at the back of Alice's neck at David's nineteenth birthday party. So why was *Constance* wearing them today? Had Alice willingly given them to her?

Before she could think it through any further, Detective Beaks came back. Being the only one left in the room that he hadn't yet talked to, his eyes rested on her.

"Your turn, Miss Banks."

She nodded and pushed away from the wall to follow him.

He took her to a small parlor and they both sat in armchairs across from one another. He studied her for a moment, one eye almost squinted.

"Could you please tell me your relationship to the deceased, Miss Constance Gilmore?"

"I don't have one."

The skeptical look on his face told her that tongues had most definitely been wagging on the topic.

"Yes, I have a history with her. Three years ago I caught her with my then-fiancé in a...compromising situation."

"That must have upset you."

"At the time it did. Now, I just have to thank her for saving me from an unfortunate marriage."

He grunted in response, obviously unconvinced. Penelope had already expected this to come up so she was hardly shaken.

"Why is it you attended this event today? Apparently, you aren't a member?"

"I was invited, and frankly somewhat bullied into coming. I'm not sure why."

"Invited? By whom?"

"Eleanor Winthorpe's aunt." She saw no reason to spare either of them.

"I see, and you were seated at the table with Miss Gilmore?"

"Yes, across from her on the other side."

"And the first to rush and help her?"

Penelope paused, her eyes narrowing with caution. "Yes, it was obvious something was wrong with her. I wanted to help."

"The woman who you once caught with your fiancé?"

"I no longer bore Constance any ill will, and I *hardly* wanted her dead. Everyone else was simply too frozen in shock."

"But not you."

"No," she said tersely.

"It seems you're a private investigator?"

"Yes," she said, her brow wrinkling at the shift in topic.

"And you've worked on cases involving murder I take it?"

"Yes," she said slowly.

"Including poison?"

"Yes, but the fact that I'm not in prison should tell you I wasn't the murderer. In fact, if you investigate it you'll find that I actually helped bring the true murderer to justice."

"But you probably learned a lot about poisons then."

"I was more focused on the suspects than the method of murder, detective."

"Right, suspects. Let's get back to today's events. It seems you disappeared before the event was to start."

Pineapples! Penelope cursed in her head.

"Only for a minute or two, and I'd hardly call it disappearing. I wandered off to explore for a bit. I'm sure Kitty—Katherine—told you that I was with her for most of that time."

"Yes," he nodded, "but only after those first few minutes."

He left out the accusation that those few minutes were quite possibly enough time to put poison in Constance's punch, which had been pre-poured by the time the luncheon started.

"Am I being accused of something, detective? Or perhaps under arrest?" She probably shouldn't have tempted him, but if the finger was being pointed at her she would have rather known sooner than later.

"No, no," he said unconvincingly, then met her with a direct gaze. "All the same, I need to ask that you remain in the city and available for further questioning."

"So I'm a suspect then?"

"Why might you be a suspect?" he asked in such a way that it encouraged her to be stupid enough to answer him.

"I suppose I should hire an attorney."

"Why would you need an attorney?"

"Is this interview over?" she snapped, realizing that they would continue down the road of leading questions.

He stared silently, no doubt hoping she would say something. Penelope just met his eyes with a level gaze.

"No further questions, Miss Banks. You're free to go.

Just bear in mind what I said about keeping yourself available for further questions."

"Yes, detective," she said tightly before rising to leave.

As she walked out of the parlor it occurred to her that perhaps there was a reason she had been chosen last for questioning beyond simply her suggesting it. She had motive and apparently, opportunity. She also had a history of being involved in a murder case involving poison. It certainly didn't look good.

This whole time, she'd been worried about the finger being unfairly pointed at someone else when it now looked as though she was the one being targeted.

Despite what she'd told Kitty it seemed she would have to take on this case after all.

CHAPTER EIGHT

PENELOPE CAUGHT UP WITH MABEL WHO WAS STILL IN the library, waiting for the police to leave.

"Mabel, can you direct me to the ladies' room?"

"Of course," Mabel said with a sympathetic smile. She probably still felt guilty about pointing Penelope out as one of the people at Constance's table. She gestured with her hand. "It's down this hallway to the left. Are you alright, dear?"

"Fine," Penelope reassured her. "Just a little shaken, of course."

"Of course. Such a tragedy," Mabel said, shaking her head and morosely looking to the side.

"It is," Penelope said, quickly escaping before the sympathies went on too long.

She didn't need to use the ladies' room, she simply needed a reason to stay long enough for the police to leave the library. But once there, she stared at herself in the mirror. Pen had never witnessed an actual death before and, despite who the victim was, it was a harrowing experience. Being accused of the crime only made it worse.

"How could they think I did it?" she quietly asked herself.

It was a stupid question. If she'd been the detective, given all the facts, she would have certainly put herself on the list. No, it wasn't the first time she'd been on such a list, but at least in prior instances, she hadn't been a serious contender. Now, she might as well have been at the top.

"Curse you, Constance," she hissed, then instantly felt ashamed of herself. Pen could hardly blame her for her own death. As much as Constance loved a good act of malice, she probably hadn't arrived today in the hopes of framing Penelope for her murder. But someone wanted her dead all the same.

Why?

Another stupid question, though perhaps less so. She had made a lot of enemies in the three years since Penelope had last seen her, but did any of them hate her enough to kill her? Motive would have to be one of the places where Penelope began. She wasn't the only person in attendance with a reason to despise Constance. And there were plenty of others with means and opportunity.

Enough time had elapsed for Penelope to assume the library was now empty. She didn't want to stay here long enough for Mabel to come knocking out of concern or suspicion. She quietly made her way back and was relieved to see that the library was all hers.

Pen wasted no time rushing over to the couch where Salvatore had settled himself. She dug around in the cushions, feeling frustrated at first when she didn't discover anything.

Maybe she'd been wrong?

She stood up, biting her lip as she stared down at the couch. She'd been certain that he'd...

"Of course!" she whispered to herself.

She dropped to her knees and looked around underneath it, almost smiling at the coincidence of finding herself in this position once again. This time was far more unpleasant. Obviously, the Peyton Foundation House didn't hire staff with the same rigidly high standards for cleaning every nook and cranny that Mrs. Winthorpe did. Through a mess of dust bunnies and other things she'd have preferred not to identify, Penelope's eyes landed on a lighter—the same gold one Constance had used earlier in the courtyard. She pulled her hand into her sleeve so as not to leave prints and grabbed it.

Penelope stared at it in thought. She clearly remembered Constance putting the gold lighter back into her purse. So how had Salvatore gotten ahold of it again?

"No wonder you were so nervous, Sal," she murmured to herself.

"Did you drop something, Miss Banks?"

Penelope quickly hid the gold lighter in her sleeved fist and turned at the sound of Mabel's voice.

"Yes, but it looks like I've found it," she said brightly as she popped up from the floor, hiding the lighter behind her back.

Mabel regarded her with curious eyes, no doubt wondering what she was doing back in the library. She may have also taken note that Penelope had been nowhere near this couch while she waited to be questioned by the detective.

Before any more suspicion could be cast upon her, Penelope headed past her, making her goodbyes. She hurried to the front door, collected her light jacket, and left, securing the lighter in one of its pockets.

It was only late afternoon and she was too eager to get

started working on this case to simply go back home and face Cousin Cordelia. It wouldn't take long for the news to spread up and down 5th Avenue and Penelope was too filled with her own anxiety to handle her cousin's delicate constitution. Hopefully, she wouldn't take too much of her "medicinal" brandy today. She'd hate to see what a completely zozzled Cousin Cordelia was like.

"What was all the hoop-a-la about? I saw a coupla police cars outside," Leonard asked after they were both back in the car, driving away.

"It seems I have another murder to solve."

He turned around to glance at her, brow understandably raised in surprise. "You really *did* go to war."

"It wasn't me," she retorted, lips pursed.

His mouth cocked into a crooked smile and he turned around to face the front again, head shaking in wonder. "So, what happened?"

"Poison."

"Again," he said softly, no doubt remembering the way Agnes, his former employer, had died.

"Yes, only this time the victim was someone I wasn't so fond of, which unfortunately has made me a prime suspect."

Once again he turned to look at her, eyes wide.

"And you thought your employment with me would be boring," she said, with a wry smile.

"So far, you have Miss Sterling beat, not something I thought I'd ever see happen."

"Welcome to the life of a lady detective. As it stands, I'll have to prioritize this case, which I haven't even been hired for, if only to clear my name."

"Whatever you need Miss Banks, I'm at your service."

She smiled at his loyalty. It disappeared when she realized where she'd need to start. A weary sigh escaped her lips.

"How do you feel about going to Times Square?"

"Another meeting so soon?"

"Call it another battle, if you will. Or perhaps an unlikely alliance. We're going to the offices of the *New York Tattle*."

She could tell that he had a hundred questions. Thankfully, he kept them to himself, which allowed Penelope to think as he drove.

The offices of the *New York Tattle* were conveniently located near Times Square. It was only appropriate that they be housed right in the muck of things, the main hub of Manhattan where everything, including the subway system, converged.

Penelope could tell they were close when the car slowed to even more of a crawl. With modern advancements in transportation, this part of town had become a bit mad with congestion. Cars, taxis, electric trolleys, and even the last remaining horse-drawn carts all fought for space, and the throng of pedestrian traffic that often paid little attention to any of it didn't help. Honks and clangs and screeching tires and shouts filled the air in a perfect cacophony that was enough to give one a headache.

As much as Penelope loved the excitement and rapid changes in her beloved city, even she found Times Square a bit much these days. At night the signs lit up enough to nearly blind you. The Paramount Building had a comically large advertisement for Clicquot Club, and the triangular Times Building had forever been a prime spot for splashy, overly-lit advertisements.

The *New York Tattle* offices were on West 47th Street near Broadway. If the owners felt any shame about the tripe that they published, the gaudy, oversized sign out front certainly didn't reflect it. There was, however, a rather intimidating man standing by the entrance ready to challenge anyone who might take issue with something that had been printed about them.

"I'm here to see Katherine Andrews. I have an appointment," she lied. Even if he checked with her, Kitty would probably still welcome Pen in, hoping for some bit of dirt to add to the article she was no doubt already writing.

"I have to check your bag," he grunted.

Penelope's brow rose slightly, but she handed her purse over. Apparently, the *New York Tattle* was more scandalous than she assumed. She could only imagine what incident had led to this bit of precaution.

After rifling through her purse, he scanned her and she had the horrid idea he would actually pat her down for weapons. Thankfully, he seemed to consider her innocent enough and instead opened the door for her.

There was a large reception desk behind which sat a pretty young woman who offered a dazzling smile as Penelope approached.

"Welcome to the *New York Tattle*, whom are you here to meet?" She asked in an overly practiced manner.

"Katherine Andrews."

"Kitty?" She said brightening up. "Should I call up and tell her you're here? We just got this new system and—"

"No, no, she's expecting me," Penelope said. The element of surprise may just work in her favor. At least this confirmed that Kitty was indeed here.

"Oh," she replied, looking deflated. Apparently, she really wanted to try that new system. "She's on the third floor."

Penelope thanked her and took the elevator up. She

exited to a large open area with about fifty desks strategically situated. Glass-fronted offices lined the walls surrounding it. Pen was surprised when her eyes landed on a mop of dark red, wavy hair attached to a woman who sat at an open desk in the very back. She would have thought someone of Kitty's privilege would have at least been afforded—or bought—a desk near the front, perhaps even an office. It seemed the Tattle was fairly egalitarian.

Kitty was tilted back in her chair, Cuban heels on the desk, legs crossed at the ankles. She was preoccupied with a notepad in her hand, brows furrowed in concentration, as though reviewing notes for the story of the year she was about to write.

Penelope quickly marched over. Kitty was so absorbed in her notes she didn't notice her at first. When she did, she nearly toppled over in her chair in surprise.

"What are you doing here?" she asked, looking embarrassed.

"I certainly hope you aren't planning on writing a story about what happened before the police have even finished their preliminary investigation. She isn't even cold yet, Kitty!"

Kitty hopped out of her chair to greet her. "Care to offer a quote?"

"Actually, I have some questions for you."

Kitty's eyes lit up. "Zounds, you *are* working on the case, aren't you?"

Penelope remained silent, giving Kitty a perfectly impassive look. But Kitty was hardly fooled.

"How about a trade?"

"Why in the world would I give you anything to splatter all over the papers?"

"Not that," Kitty said with a dismissive wave of the

hand. She looked around, noting the other people at their desks and a cautious look came to her face. She reached out and took Penelope's wrist to drag her into an empty office. After closing the door she let go and turned to face her again.

"I want in on your case, I want to be a part of it, see how a real female private detective works."

"I'm hardly the one to look to, I've only been in business for a few months and even then, I've only had one newsworthy case."

"But it was a doozy though," Kitty replied with a grin, not at all dissuaded as Pen had hoped. "And this one will be even bigger. Let's not pretend you won't be working on it, mostly because I'd be willing to bet the police are already homing in on you as suspect number one."

"What did you tell them?" Pen asked, eyes narrowed.

"Nothing but the truth," Kitty said, holding her hand up as though swearing on a Bible. Her bottom lip protruded and she gave her a pointed look as she continued. "Because you are in fact a detective, and everyone knows you helped with Agnes Sterling's murder. Also, you were missing for a good five minutes, during which you could have done anything—like poison Constance's drink. If it makes you feel better about working with me, the detective already had that bit confirmed by someone else by the time he got to me."

Once again, Penelope remained silent on the heels of that, not wanting to give Kitty anything she could potentially use against her. She also didn't want to point out that she still considered Kitty a suspect as well. Working with her wouldn't just give her this much-needed information about what was said at the table, Kitty might very well reveal something to reveal her own culpability.

"I can see some persuasion is in order," she said with a smirk. "Okay, let me lay it out for you Penelope Banks, you need information from me, something to point the finger at someone else."

"I have no interest in framing anyone if that's what you're insinuating."

"Perish the thought!" Kitty scoffed with exaggerated indignation. "However, you're not the only one with a potential motive for murder. Constance was notoriously hated, mostly because she knew everyone's secrets. Now that she's dead, I'm one of the few people who also know those secrets, all of which gave everyone at that table a motive for murder."

It was tempting, too tempting. But Penelope was still loath to work with Kitty, mostly because of where she worked.

"The fact is, you need me, Pen. They're hardly likely to confide in you themselves, no matter how much you pressure them. It's better to have the information beforehand as a form of ammunition when you approach them."

Pen hated that she was right. "What is it you get out of this?"

"The stories as they unravel of course."

"Absolutely not! You printing every little revelation would be disastrous. I've seen firsthand how easy it is to go down the perilous road of assuming someone is guilty, only to be proven wrong."

"Fine, I'll only publish if it's a proven fact."

"And taint the jury ahead of time? No."

Kitty's mouth twisted in irritation. "This isn't going to work."

Penelope considered her. "Yes, it can. I see a way for it to work out for both of us."

CHAPTER NINE

"You want to be taken seriously as a journalist," Penelope said to Kitty. "It's quite obvious you were hoping your connections and working here, spilling all of the upper crust secrets, would be a segue into that world, but it hasn't happened so far."

The way Kitty's cheeks reddened and her eyes narrowed told Penelope she had guessed correctly. She soldiered on.

"This story is big, you already know that, which is why you came straight here after the fact. The trial, when it happens, could be even bigger. Perhaps even enough to land a position at the *New York Times*."

There was a brief spark in Kitty's eyes at the mention of that publication. "What do you expect from me?" she asked warily.

"Save any publication until at least the start of the trial."

Kitty coughed out an incredulous laugh. "Impossible. Do you know how the news works? Specifically the *New York Tattle*?"

"I do know what happens to journalists who are accused of defamation and libel."

"Which is exactly why I plan on using you for information. Surely any detective worth their salt would only uncover the truth?" she replied tartly.

"You're right, this isn't going to work," Penelope sighed and looked off to the side. "And to think, there could be an entire full-page spread on this, walking readers through the entire history of the case, complete with insider knowledge. Perhaps even a book. But you insist on limiting yourself to the *New York Tattle*."

The hungry look on Kitty's face told Pen her ambitions were indeed higher. Still, she could understand the hesitation. The lure of the still very recent murder, and being on the scene when it occurred was a story that was aching to be published.

"I have to get today's story in. My editor will fire me if I don't."

"Heavens, however will you get by?" Pen said with a dry look.

"I take my job as seriously as you do," she retorted. "But, you do have a point. Perhaps I *would* like to advance in this career."

"So be patient, go after a much bigger story for a much bigger reward. Do that much and I'll give you full access. Or as much as those I talk to will allow."

Kitty was set to object but Pen cut her off.

"Trust is an important part of what I do. If people feel as though everything they say will be splashed across the front page the next day, they'll never tell me anything. Then you'll have no story at all for your efforts."

Kitty, so used to leaping without looking seemed to be

struggling over this, but something Pen had said apparently stuck.

"Alright, deal." She stuck her hand out and Pen shook it. "After I publish today's story."

Penelope hesitated but realized whatever was published today was going to happen no matter what, and wouldn't be terribly harmful.

"Deal," Pen ceded, shaking Kitty's hand. "Now, what are these secrets?"

"Oh no, you don't. If we're going to do this, we do it properly. Allow me to submit my story, then we'll go back to your office. I want every bit of the experience of being a lady private detective."

"Jane, this is Katherine Andrews," Penelope said when they entered her office. "She goes by Kitty."

Pen wasn't surprised when her newly minted assistant Jane Pugley greeted their guest formally. "How do you do, Miss Andrews?"

"It's Kitty. Nice to meet you, Jane," Kitty said, her eyes scanning the office. "Swanky. I should hire your decorator."

The office was done in the recent Art Deco style, mostly black and gold geometric lines and shapes, with plenty of chrome on display. Pen thought it rather fitting for a professional office, especially for a woman such as herself who appreciated aesthetically pleasing touches.

"We have yet another important case to work on, Jane, probably the most important we'll have ever."

"Our Pen has been accused of murder," Kitty blurted with a gleeful vigor.

Penelope sighed, irritated at having that bit revealed

in such a casual manner. Sure enough, Jane's eyes went wide with alarm. Despite having been a major part of Pen's last case, which became quite dangerous toward the end, she was still rather skittish about certain things like this. Still, she had at least fired a gun at someone in Penelope's defense, so Pen knew she could rely on her in a pinch.

She briefly explained to Jane what had happened at the luncheon.

"Don't worry," Pen assured her, making sure to give Kitty a glare, "I obviously haven't murdered anyone. However, I am unfortunately a suspect. What we need to do is work out who the *real* killer is."

"Anything you need, Miss Banks," Jane said instantly, loyal as ever.

"Kitty here is going to help us unravel some motives other suspects might have. As you well know, this job sometimes means dealing with unsavory characters."

"I've been called worse," Kitty said with a note of pride in her voice. She flopped down on the chair across from Pen's desk. "So where do we begin?"

"We'll begin with you finally revealing what was going on at lunch," Penelope said, taking the seat across from her. She turned to Jane with a grim smile. "Please make sure to have your pencil and notepad ready."

"Ah yes, all the dirty secrets," Kitty said with a grin. She sat up straighter, suddenly alert with focus. "Let's start with the one who fully expected to be chairlady of the Young Ladies Historical Preservation Society, a position she lost by exactly one vote as I said."

"Marie Phillips?"

"Yes, here's one of those unverified facts that you won't find me printing in the *New York Tattle*."

"It's nice to know the paper does have some standards," Penelope said dryly.

"Hate it all you want, but they *do* in fact have standards. They also have an entire law firm on retainer, including their very own in-house counsel to keep them from getting sued," she said, with a note of irritation in her voice.

"What is this unverified fact?"

"That Constance and Marie had a wager going. The winner of the position as chair of the Young Ladies Historical Preservation Society would get a spring wedding."

Penelope stared for a moment wondering if there was more. "*That's it?*"

"You scoff, but for some young ladies weddings are everything," Kitty said loftily.

"So, Marie lost a spring wedding and the position of chair, which I also assume she wanted?"

"Very much so. As I said, I can't *verify* the fact that a bet was made. However, I *can* verify that five hundred pink tulips were planted in the gardens of the Kilgore Club in Long Island just before the election for chairlady took place in late October. Tulips and pink are Marie's favorites. In fact, they should be blooming within the next two weeks. A shame."

Penelope knew better than to suggest that Marie simply hold her wedding a few weeks before or after Constance's. There was only one society wedding per season, one per year if it was to be a particularly grand affair, and Constance would have made sure it was. Marie would have had to wait until at least summer when it was hot and muggy or fall when neither pink nor tulips would be appropriate. Winter was out of the question.

"You know Constance. As soon as she saw Marie engaged, she had to do the same, and then turn the entire thing into a competition. I'm almost certain she didn't even care about either a spring wedding or being chair until she saw that Marie was vying for both."

"Poor Marie," Jane lamented. "This Constance sounds positively horrid."

"And then some."

"You could say that."

Both Kitty and Penelope had spoken at the same time and met each other with wry looks. Kitty turned back to Jane, a slow smile spreading her mouth as it occurred to her that the name was unfamiliar to her.

"No, she doesn't know about my history with Constance," Penelope preempted. "And *I'd* prefer to be the one to tell her."

Kitty shrugged and sat back in her chair.

"I was once engaged to a man named Clifford Stokes. The day before our wedding, I caught Constance and him... together in a rather intimate way." Jane gasped in surprise, but Pen quickly continued. The last thing she wanted was pity. "I broke off the engagement then and there. My father was unhappy with me and cut me off. For three years, I had to make it mostly on my own, with very few friends to help me." She cast a quick, pointed look Kitty's way before turning back to Jane. "At least until Agnes Sterling left me the five million in kale. *That* is my history with Constance."

"And exactly why the police think maybe your boss may have killed her," Kitty said in a dramatically somber voice.

"Even though there were several others who may have had motive," Penelope said, pointedly arching her eyebrow at Kitty.

"Yes, yes, moving on to the next suspect on the list, our little darling Alice, otherwise known as Constance's Sisyphus."

"Sisyphus?" Jane asked.

"From Greek mythology. He was forced to roll a boulder up a hill only to have it roll down again and again," Pen explained. She turned her attention back to Kitty. "What did Constance have on Alice?"

"That she has an absolute crush on one of the workmen who helped build their house in Newport."

"A crush?" Jane asked in confusion.

"Goodness Jane, how old are you?" Kitty scolded, even though she was around the same age as Pen and Kitty. "I feel as though I'm talking to my Aunt Claris. Smitten. Besotted. Enamored."

"Yes, yes, she gets it," Pen said, rolling her eyes.

Kitty continued with a laugh. "Of course, the Todds had to fire the entire work crew. But that certainly hasn't stopped the two of them from sneaking away to make whoopee."

"Whoopee?" Jane asked, even though she was already blushing.

Pen allowed Kitty to do the explaining again, mostly because her mind had reversed back to the pearls. Had Alice given Constance the pearls to keep her quiet?

"That hardly seems worthy of blackmail," Penelope said doubtfully.

"Well, when you're Alice Todd, almost anything could be blackmail."

That much rang true. Even as a young girl Alice aimed to please everyone around her if only to avoid even a hint of scorn, admonishment, or discord.

"Could someone like her even commit murder?"

"A dog who is kicked enough will eventually bite back," Kitty said with a shrug.

There was something to be said for that as well.

"What about Eleanor?" Penelope was eager to learn more about the young woman who had invited her in the first place. Hopefully whatever Kitty had to say about her might clarify things.

"She and John Duke were once nearly engaged. In fact, they *were,* for all intents and purposes, until Constance stepped into the picture."

"*What?*"

Both Jane and Penelope exclaimed at the same time.

No wonder John had been so uncomfortable at the luncheon. Being in the same room as his current fiancée and the girl he had once intended to marry? It also explained why the Dukes had left so suddenly.

Kitty giggled at having surprised them. "Pen, you should know better than anyone, she likes stealing other girls' toys, or should I say, boys."

"In this case, she decided to get engaged to said boy."

"In this case, both fathers insisted."

"Constance isn't...?" Penelope left the question open to the most obvious interpretation.

"Pregnant?" Kitty went ahead and finished for her.

Jane inhaled sharply next to her.

Kitty laughed as she answered, amused she'd scandalized Jane. "That would be entirely *too* much of a scandal, even for our Constance. No, she took him from Eleanor, who dropped him right after her birthday last year. I'm not exactly sure what led John to Constance of all people, being that it was obvious he still pined for Eleanor. He at least had the grace to wait a couple of months after the breakup to go running into Constance's arms.

"Still, both the Gilmores and the Dukes decided it was a fine match. It does have a sort of congruency. I mean, you don't get ownership of the most viable rail lines in the city without cozying up to a few politicians. The Gilmores have infiltrated the government at almost every level. I wouldn't be surprised to see a President Gilmore in the future. Even I have to admit it's an ideal match."

"At least before Constance was murdered," Penelope reminded her. "But getting back to Eleanor Winthorpe, she didn't seem particularly upset at lunch."

"Eleanor Winthorpe showing any hint of emotion would be like the Yankees not winning the pennant."

Penelope was well aware of the popularity of baseball, but she was hardly a fan. At the blank looks from Jane and Pen, Kitty gave an exaggerated sigh and rolled her eyes.

"What I'm saying is, it isn't in Eleanor's nature to show emotion. I'm almost certain there's lizard blood running through those veins of hers, or at the very least ice."

"So, you sat her at the table to see if she'd melt?"

"Or just to rattle Constance. She deserves a good hard shake, wouldn't you agree?"

Penelope refrained from answering. Eleanor's "secret" wasn't all that tantalizing or illuminating, in retrospect. To be fair, neither were the others. Still, despite having the temperament of an insouciant cat, it didn't mean Eleanor wasn't still seething inside at having John Duke stolen by Constance.

"Do you have any more information about Eleanor?" Penelope prodded hopefully.

"Eleanor might as well be a vault. Nothing escapes, which is ironic considering her father owns half the newspapers in the country. Hmm, maybe it's because of that." She added with a shrug.

"I noticed she and Constance had similar scarves on. Is there anything to that?"

"Constance wears it to every event she knows Eleanor

will also be attending. I honestly assumed Eleanor had thrown hers away because of it."

"Constance was also wearing Alice's pearls, the ones that matched the earrings Alice had on."

Kitty smirked. "You're catching on. Constance likes to rub things in, a little more salt in the wound. She was always wearing Alice's pearls at meetings. Notice she was in pink as well? It's Marie's favorite color, one she basically gave up for these meetings. I have to say, Marie doesn't look quite as in the, ah, pink of health wearing yellow. Constance certainly knows where to aim the dart."

That was Constance through and through. "How does she have so much to hold against everyone? Where does she get her information? Likewise, how is it you know what you do?"

"It's my job, Pen."

Pen simply arched an eyebrow and waited.

"Truly! If you don't think I put in the work, then that just shows how much you know about me. I have no idea how Constance knows what she does. I doubt she works as hard as I do."

"But she knows things all the same." Penelope narrowed her eyes. "And just what is it Constance had on you, Katherine?"

CHAPTER TEN

Kitty stared back at Penelope, all hints of humor and amusement vanishing.

"Did you think I missed the remark Constance made about you supposedly *saying something you'd have to take back*? It did a fine job of silencing you. You didn't honestly think I'd leave it alone, did you?"

"It was nothing," Kitty said, her jaw tightening.

"Which should make it easy for you to tell me."

Jane's eyes danced back and forth between the two of them as she held her pencil ready.

Kitty exhaled a puff of air, then dramatically waved her hands as though it wasn't much of a bother for her to reveal what Constance knew about her.

"There...may have been an article I almost ran that suggested certain New York aldermen were taking bribes. The source I had reneged on what he had told me, claiming I made the entire thing up. Though, I'm almost certain he was paid off or threatened. Still, the whole thing was handled quietly and there was no harm done."

"The *New York Tattle* still kept you on the paper after that?"

"Only because it was caught in time prior to publication. It isn't as though I didn't suffer any consequences because of it," Kitty snapped in a bitter tone.

Penelope suspected her desk in the very back part of the open floor of the *New York Tattle* was her punishment. She imagined Kitty having to walk past the desks of more seasoned gossip mongers every day, her head held down in shame, and *almost* felt sorry for her.

"Do you suspect Constance was the one to set you up?"

"I don't have proof of that," Kitty said, but her burning eyes narrowed into slits, which told Penelope that she did indeed suspect Constance was behind it.

"That sounds like a perfect motive for murder," Penelope suggested.

"Almost as much as finding her in a compromising position with the man you're set to marry the next day," Kitty spat back.

Penelope smiled. "This isn't as much fun as you thought it would be, is it? Being the subject of scandal and gossip."

"Horsefeathers, I'm having a gloriously wonderful time," Kitty sang, the sarcasm in her voice drenching every word.

"Was there anyone else there who might have done it?" Jane interjected in some attempt to make peace.

Both Kitty and Penelope glared at each other for a moment longer before relenting. Kitty turned to Jane with a sigh and said, "If there is one thing I know about Constance, it's that she liked to control almost everyone around her. I doubt a single girl in that room was immune."

"But only a few had access to her glass of punch," Penelope said, staring off to the side in thought. She suddenly stood up, her mind going to work. "Actually, I think that's what we should focus on."

"What? Access to her glass?" Kitty asked, perking up as well as she watched Penelope pace back and forth.

"Exactly."

"That does make sense," Kitty said.

"Starting with you," Penelope said with a wry smile.

Kitty frowned, which gave Pen a fleeting sense of satisfaction.

Penelope looked around. "We need a blackboard is what. It would make plotting this out so much easier."

"I can have one bought and delivered," Jane said. "I'll inquire at the nearby schools about what company they use to order theirs."

Penelope graced her with an appreciative smile. "What would I do without you?" She was pleased to see the glow of pleasure emanating from Jane.

"In the meantime, I have my notepad." Jane lifted it.

"That will have to do. In fact, now that I think about it, you can serve another use. It will be good to describe in detail the entire event to someone who wasn't there. You can pose questions and make observations we wouldn't think of."

"Like what was Pen doing during those five minutes she disappeared?" Kitty said with a smug smirk.

"Or what else Kitty was up to while she was rearranging the place cards?" Penelope retorted.

"Are you two going to fight this entire time?" Jane asked, with mild exasperation.

Pen was surprised and somewhat impressed at her assistant's patronizing tone. She reminded herself to encourage it in the future. Even Penelope needed to be put in her place every once in a while, if only to stay focused.

"No, we're going to be perfectly factual, even if it paints us in a bad light," Penelope said, giving Kitty a hard stare.

Kitty shrugged and offered a pert smile. "I promise to play nice."

"Okay," Penelope continued, taking a breath as she resumed pacing. "You were there before I got there. Did you see anyone go into the room where lunch was served?"

"No, but I can say the punch hadn't yet been poured when I went in to switch the cards."

Penelope stopped and gave her a thoughtful look. "Did you change Constance's card?"

Kitty shook her head. "Only Constance and Alice were originally supposed to be at that table. I changed Alice's location at the table, but everyone, including you, was originally seated elsewhere."

"Which means the glass at her place setting was always hers. If the poison was potent enough, a small, barely noticeable dose could have been added before the punch was served."

"Which opens the pool of potential suspects up even wider. Do you honestly think we were the only ones targeted by Constance? I simply sat the most obvious nemeses at her table, the ones I knew she either took issue with or was blackmailing. If I had to guess, I'd say there were more suspects at other tables."

Penelope brought her hand up to her head, feeling the pounding begin. "Let's just...work under the assumption the poison was added after the punch was served."

"Which absolves me!" Kitty happily quipped.

"For the moment," Pen said, giving her a dour look.

She continued pacing.

"So, after you changed the place cards, Alice escorted

the two Dukes in." She stopped to consider that. "I suppose we should add them to the list of suspects."

"Oh, this is getting even more delicious," Kitty said in an excited tone. She turned to Jane. "That is, John Duke, Constance's fiancé, and Samuel Duke, his father."

Jane dutifully wrote the names down, though her brow rose a bit at the idea that they could be potential suspects as well.

"You wouldn't happen to know any gossip about them would you?"

"The only suspicious thing about them is why they are so set on saving this house of theirs. I know they aren't in real estate, but I would have thought Samuel of all people would at least be smart enough to tear down a useless old house to erect an apartment building on it. Turning it into some kind of private club seems like a waste."

Penelope mulled that over and, while Kitty had a point about it being a waste, she couldn't really tie that to a reason for murdering Constance. After all, she was working with her future in-laws toward their goals, as odd as they were.

"We have to add Alice to the list, Jane."

"Wait a second, you completely skipped over the moment when you disappeared," Kitty accused.

"You're right," Pen said diplomatically. "Jane, in the timeline, be sure to mark that before the Dukes arrived, I had a brief moment to myself. Call it ten minutes just to be overly cautious." She turned to Kitty with an expectant look.

"That's fair."

"Now that I think about it, there was also the moment when Salvatore and Constance disappeared. If they separated it would have given him an opportunity to come inside and slip poison into her drink." She twisted her lips to the side, imagining it. "Unlikely, but I don't want to rule anyone out."

Out of all the suspects, he'd probably be the easiest to interrogate, especially with the gold lighter she had as leverage. But she wasn't about to tell Kitty any of this.

"Speaking of the help, those Bolshevik waiters should definitely go on the list. I imagine murdering the chairlady of a group trying to protect a Park Avenue Mansion fits right in with their diabolical aims."

"That's an unfair judgment," Penelope scolded.

"Did you see what they did to the royal family in Russia? I'm surprised we weren't *all* poisoned!"

"An accusation which only makes them look less guilty. Why ruin their message with murder?" Penelope pointed out. "But yes, they should go on the list if we're to be completely egalitarian."

"Something they'd ironically appreciate," Kitty said in a dry voice.

"Moving on," Pen said. "Eleanor was the first from our table to enter. I remember that much."

"We're forgetting Mabel!" Kitty said. "She was the one to open the doors fully. She must have entered from the side door as the waiters did."

Penelope nodded in acknowledgment. "True. But do we even have a motive?"

"Having to deal with Constance at every gathering of the Young Ladies Historical Preservation Society would be enough for me."

"She seems a tad more level-headed than that," Penelope said. "Still, she does belong on the list, Jane. Perhaps a motive will come to light as we investigate. After that, Eleanor entered, so that would give her an opportunity to poison the punch before the other members of our table were seated."

"And that's the crop. After this, we were all seated at the table," Kitty said throwing up her hands.

"No, it doesn't end there. Who's to say that the poison wasn't added after that? There was the period when Mr. Duke was speaking."

"Yes! And that incident with the waiter and Marie," Kitty added.

"The incident with the onions?" Jane clarified as she scribbled on her pad.

"Yes, Marie got into an argument with the entitled Bolshevik," Kitty said.

"It was a brief but terse discussion before he took her plate away," Pen corrected, giving Kitty an exasperated look.

"That probably still drew attention away from Constance's glass," Jane pointed out.

"Except Marie was sitting right next to Constance. Surely someone would have seen it happen if they were focused on her?" Kitty said doubtfully.

"I've seen sleights of hand that would amaze you," Penelope said. "And she was waving her hand pretty wildly. We should certainly factor that incident in."

"Okay, then what?" Jane asked after jotting it down.

"Then Kitty began her round of teasing each of our table mates," Pen said, shooting an accusatory glance her way.

"And Constance continued where I left off," Kitty needled right back. "Focusing most of her barbs on our dear Penelope. Though I have to give it to your boss, she gave as good as she got. In fact, I think most people at the table would agree, you won that fight, Pen."

"*Then*," Penelope continued, ignoring that. "Constance drank her punch, and...died."

"Oh," Jane said sadly, though she wrote it down.

Penelope decided the details of Constance's death toward the end wouldn't help discover a motive or a guilty party, so she spared Jane.

Still, there was something about those final moments that nagged at Penelope. Something that didn't quite fit with everything she had learned just now.

She realized it was the pearls, the pink pearls that matched the ones in Alice's ears. They were the problem. Why was Alice wearing her earrings? Had Constance forced her to? It seemed to add insult to injury. Of course, Constance seemed to have no limit to her cruelty, even when it came to such an easy target like Alice.

Before she could express these thoughts, there was a knock on the front door of the office.

Jane hopped up from her chair to open the door. When she escorted their guest in, her face was already glowing with delight.

"Detective Prescott? Well, I must really be in trouble if I've earned a visit from you," Penelope said, mostly teasing, though she could feel her heartbeat quicken ever so slightly just from being in the same room as him.

"I'm afraid you might just be, Miss Banks."

CHAPTER ELEVEN

"And just who is this?" Kitty asked in a coy voice as her eyes darted back and forth between Penelope and Detective Richard Prescott.

Her slightly flirtatious manner was understandable. He was quite handsome with sharp features and dark eyes surrounded by full lashes. The only flaw, though Penelope somewhat adored it, was the burn scar that started at the lower half of the right side of his face down to the neck—a souvenir from the Great War. Looking at him straight on, one could just barely see it.

"This is Detective Richard Prescott, we...worked on a case together," Penelope said dismissively. She wanted to know what he meant just now that she might be in trouble.

"I'm Katherine Andrews, but everyone calls me Kitty." She jumped up and held out her hand, greeting the detective with a smile that perfectly matched her nickname.

"Pleasure to meet you," he said, dragging his eyes away from Pen long enough to offer a tight smile and shake Kitty's hand. He let go and instantly turned his attention back to Penelope.

"Are you here to arrest me?" Penelope asked in alarm.

"No," he said quickly, "I just..." He sighed and ran his hand over his thick dark hair. It was a sign of his frustration, Penelope had learned. She tensed, awaiting what he would say. He met her eyes with a direct stare. "They won't make an arrest until they're sure, not with someone of your stature. Anyone else..."

"They would have dragged me down to the precinct."

He nodded grimly. "Most likely."

"And you've come because...?" She was still confused.

"I...wanted to see how you were. Is this the first murder you've witnessed firsthand?"

Her eyelashes fluttered in surprise. "You came just to see how I am?"

"Well, yes. I know we have a history of crossing swords, but that doesn't mean I don't feel a certain—"

"Adoration," she said, with a smile, unable to help herself despite the circumstances.

"Concern for your well-being," he said, mildly irritated. It made her smile even more.

Jane, beside him, beamed even more brightly. She revered Detective Prescott, almost like an affectionate puppy.

Kitty, on the other hand, looked as though she had stepped into something perfectly scandalous. She didn't bother hiding the salacious look on her face. Penelope ignored it.

"I'm fine, thank you, Detective Prescott," Penelope said. She had been tempted to use his first name, just to tease him even more, but knew the circumstances—especially with Kitty here—didn't warrant it. He was always such a stickler for maintaining strict professionalism. "Though I would be even better if you told me what you know exactly?"

"As you might imagine, this case has been made a priority. It's not my precinct, but I have friends in all the station houses, and I received a courtesy call, being that our association is well known."

He didn't look at all pleased about that fact. Penelope had the idea that their association was more notorious than anything, especially after the last case.

"What I do know is that a preliminary exam indicates it was poison and that it came from the punch she drank. They'll need to run more tests to discover exactly what the poison was."

"Yes, I assumed as much," Penelope said with a sigh.

Detective Prescott nodded. "What I really came to say was that there is quite a bit of pressure to make an arrest. There are also a lot of people pointing the finger at you. Honestly, after your run-in with the law from the last case, you don't have a lot of friends on the police force, at least not among the higher-ups."

Penelope bristled somewhat, annoyed that her attempts —successful attempts!—at bringing justice to light would be rewarded with such animosity.

"It's now Wednesday. I suspect there will be an arrest by the end of the week, no later than Friday."

"And that arrest is likely to be me," she finished for him, feeling her heart stop beating for a few seconds.

"The direction it seems to be going, I'm afraid it may be. Unless something new develops."

"I see," she said.

Jane looked petrified. Even Kitty gave Pen a solemn look.

"What do you need from me?" he asked so ardently, it made Penelope's heart begin beating again, now twice as fast. "I assume you'll be working on the case?"

"It would be imprudent if I wasn't, don't you think?"

A humorless smile came to his face. "You have my telephone number. Don't hesitate to use it. So long as I'm not interfering in an ongoing investigation," he cautioned, because of course he would. He was a stickler for that as well.

"Thank you, Detective Prescott."

"Of course, Miss Banks." He nodded, gave her one last look, which hinted that he wanted to say something more. His eyes flicked to Kitty and he simply nodded again then said quick goodbyes to the other two and left.

"My, what a dashing fellow!" Kitty announced with a teasing smile. "A shame about the scar, he could have been a star in the movies. He could certainly put good old Rudolph to shame."

"Perhaps you missed the reason why he made the visit?" Penelope said in a terse voice.

"Yes, of course," Kitty said, at least having the tact to look abashed. Her eyes brightened once again. "What are you going to do? You have two, maybe three days before they slap you in nippers."

"I'll have to work faster and harder, which means not putting everything else off." She rose to leave.

Unfortunately, Kitty took note. "Where to? Remember we're supposed to be working together!"

Pen was tempted to lie, but she had made a deal. Besides, Kitty might inadvertently prove useful.

"Fine, but remember I'm the investigator here. And keep in mind that I still haven't ruled you out as a suspect."

Kitty grinned. "Nor I you, so I suppose that makes us equals. So, where to, Sherlock?"

"Back to the scene of the crime. I have to clear something up."

CHAPTER TWELVE

"Back to the scene of the crime, I see," Leonard said, echoing Penelope's earlier statement as he parked the car in front of Peyton Foundation House.

"If I'm to avoid going to prison, I have no choice," Penelope said with a sigh.

Kitty, who had kept her eyes on Penelope's chauffeur during the entire ride, obviously enjoying what she saw, now grinned, excited at the prospect of joining in.

"Don't worry, she won't give me details either," she said prettily as Leonard opened the door and held out a hand to help her out of the car. He grinned back in a way that had Penelope grimacing with annoyance. Heaven help him if he entertained any ideas with Kitty.

The Peyton Foundation House wasn't Pen's first choice of places to start—she desperately wanted to speak with both Alice and Eleanor for different reasons—but she knew this would be the path of much less resistance. She might as well eliminate all other avenues before fighting an uphill battle with the Todds and Winthorpes, perhaps eventually even the Phillips. After all, when it came to Constance

Gilmore, there was no shortage of reasons one might have murderous intentions.

"It looks like such a harmless place on the outside," Kitty remarked as they walked to the front door. "One would never have suspected murder took place here only a few hours ago."

"Any place is capable of being a setting for murder."

She pressed the electric door buzzer. After a moment Mabel opened it.

"Miss Banks. Miss Andrews," she greeted in surprise.

"Penelope, please," she reminded her, hoping that would earn her some goodwill.

"And please call me Kitty as well," her "partner" added in a chummy tone.

"Of course," Mabel said distractedly as she opened the door wider for them to enter. "Thankfully, the police have left. Did you forget something? I know with all the...well, you know, it would have been easy to get distracted. I should warn you that they have forbidden anyone to enter the room where the luncheon was held. It is still considered a crime scene."

"Actually, I was hoping to speak with the gardener. Salvatore Rizzo was his name?"

Kitty flashed her eyes to Penelope in surprise but thankfully kept quiet.

Mabel's hand came up to her chest to fiddle with the collar of her dress. "Salvatore? Whatever for?"

"It's...personal," Penelope said, lowering her eyelids with faux embarrassment. She doubted Constance was the only young lady who had dabbled with the affections of the gardener, as handsome as he was.

Mabel became flustered, realizing how intrusive the question had been. Penelope was fine with her thinking sordid thoughts so long as she was able to get a moment to speak with him.

"I'm afraid he left as soon as the questioning was over. And he only comes once a week, so he won't be back until next Wednesday."

"Oh," Penelope said, disappointed. "It's a shame, I had something of his to return to him."

"I see," Mabel said, reclaiming her decorum. "Well, perhaps I could hold it for him. That is if it isn't too personal."

Penelope wasn't about to hand over the gold lighter and add a third person to this mess. It was bad enough having to be transparent with Kitty. She thought of another ruse.

"Actually, as it turns out, the apartment building I live in is thinking of getting some work done for our own courtyard. Does he work with a company that services gardens around the city? Or perhaps it's his own business?"

"He works for his uncle's company. They do work with a number of clients around the city. In fact, Salvatore was recommended to me by someone else who was quite pleased with his service."

Kitty inadvertently snorted next to Penelope and she gave her a sharp look of rebuke.

"I have the information on file somewhere. That's awfully kind of you to consider him. I have to say, he works wonders with our garden. If you'll give me a moment?"

"Thank you," Penelope replied graciously.

When she was gone, Kitty couldn't help herself.

"He works wonders with my garden," she mimicked in a whisper before breaking out in laughter. She added with waggling eyebrows, "I wonder how many other gardens he has serviced in this city."

"If you're going to behave like a child, I'll have to leave

you with Jane to babysit next time I venture out," she hissed. "This is a *murder* investigation. One that happened only a few hours ago?"

Kitty instantly composed herself, appropriately abashed.

Penelope sighed and wandered over to the library to look out at 4th Avenue. The moment of peaceful solitude was interrupted by the sound of the trolley clanging as it started up from its stop. She winced at the grating sound of it and turned away to admire the stained glass on the doors once again.

"Hmm, a René Gauthier."

Penelope gave Kitty a look of surprise.

"What? I'm not a complete Luddite," Kitty scoffed.

"A lovely design, isn't it?"

Penelope and Kitty turned at the sound of Mabel's voice as she came back.

"Not original to this house, of course, this home was built long before the art nouveau movement. These doors were included later on by yet another chairlady of the Young Ladies Historical Preservation Society almost twenty years ago, long before I began working here. I know at least a few matrons would love to get their hands on these for various museums or new homes being built."

"It makes a lovely addition to this house."

"Yes, not all progress needs to be grandiose." Mabel looked around the interior. "Sadly, I fear Peyton Foundation House may be the next victim of the current real estate race to build bigger and taller buildings."

"Is there a threat to tear this place down?" Penelope asked.

Mabel laughed lightly, but there was a hint of uncertainty. "Fortunately, 4th Avenue isn't quite yet fashionable.

Still, one never knows which neighborhood will become the next most desirable address for the wealthy. There are only so many avenues in Manhattan to build on. Who knows? One day it may be the meatpacking district."

"The Meatpacking District?" Penelope said with an incredulous laugh. "That's nothing but slaughterhouses." She shuddered at the idea of living amid all that viscera and carnage.

"It was once quite a desirable area for many; a very convenient location, after all. It's right next to Greenwich Village which is quite the bohemian experience I understand. That's the thing about this city, it moves in waves and cycles. Right now no one is paying much attention to 4th Avenue, but if you go north a few blocks, Park Avenue is all the rage."

Mabel sighed with resignation as she continued. "Which is why the Young Ladies Historical Preservation Society was such an asset. Places like the Duke Home, while they may not serve much of a practical purpose, they at least serve as reminders of what this city once was, the quaint beauty of it appeals to one's sensibilities."

"I suppose," Penelope said diplomatically. She herself thought perhaps quaint beauty was a luxury that probably wouldn't mean much to families packed into tenement buildings. The way this city's population was growing, taller and bigger was where the future was headed, which was probably a good thing. Though one wondered just how tall they could go. The Woolworth Building was already an awe-inspiring 60 stories high.

Still, she felt for Mabel. Relics like Peyton Foundation House might very well be one of the victims of progress.

"Of course, it is tragic to lose Constance beyond just her service as chairlady for the Society," Mabel quickly added.

"I certainly don't want to give the impression that I only care about the cause she was dedicated to."

"I didn't think such a thing at all," Penelope assured her.

While Penelope hadn't cared for Constance, she certainly wouldn't have wished her dead. She could only imagine how a more neutral party would feel, seeing someone die, especially in such an inelegant manner.

Kitty cleared her throat. "You said you had an address for the gardener?"

"I'm sorry," Mabel said, quickly shaking her head and smiling as she handed over a slip of paper. "Yes, this is the company Salvatore works for. I'm sure they'll be glad of the business. Unfortunately, private gardens are also falling prey to progress as well."

"Thank you," Penelope said, giving the stained glass doors and 4th Avenue beyond it one last look before leaving.

CHAPTER THIRTEEN

The address that Mabel had given was on Mulberry Street, which wasn't a surprise. Many Italian Americans lived in that part of New York City, and a company that went by the name Giordano Landscaping was probably right at home there. How the Peyton Foundation House had come to hire them was the real surprise, especially if it was at the recommendation of any of the wealthy families in this city.

At any rate, it was impossible for Leonard to get the car onto the street, being so filled with stands and vendors selling their wares. Penelope insisted he let them out on Grand Street instead.

"Are you sure, Miss Banks?" He asked giving the neighborhood a doubtful look as he opened the door for them.

"We'll be fine. What could possibly happen to us here? Besides, it's still afternoon."

"It looks like fun!" Kitty added with a grin as she bounded out of the car after her. "I love scouring different parts of the city like this. So different from the Upper East Side, no?"

For once, Penelope agreed with her. This was a vibrant part of the city that spoke to how unique and colorful it was. No doubt much to the chagrin of women like Mrs. Winthorpe.

Around them, were people going about their day, running errands or making deliveries. The entire street was a busy hive of activity. And yes, far different from the quiet serenity further north in the neighborhoods bordering Central Park.

Giordano Landscaping had a storefront near the southern part of the street. They entered to find it filled with gardening supplies for sale. An older man behind the counter perked up at the sound of the door opening, then saw who it was that walked in. Two young ladies still dressed for a society luncheon probably weren't the typical clientele who visited his store.

"Can I help you?" he greeted with polite uncertainty and a definite accent.

"Yes, I was hoping to speak with one of your gardeners, Salvatore Rizzo?" Pen said.

Instantly the pleasantly polite look on his face transformed into one of exasperated irritation. "What has that nephew of mine done now?"

"Oh, he's not in any trouble," Penelope said quickly. "I just have something to return to him."

He studied them with a different eye, one that certainly assumed certain things. He was tactful enough to refrain from actually saying anything.

"He's in the back, I will get him."

"He probably thinks there's some sordid love triangle going on," Kitty mused once he was gone.

"You can leave any time."

"Horsefeathers, I'm curious to see which of us Salvatore will choose," she teased.

Salvatore strode in, his tongue rolling in his cheek. It reminded Penelope of a child who knew they had misbehaved but also knew the punishment would be nothing more than a slap on the back of the hand from an indulgent parent.

Up close he was even more handsome than what she'd seen of him earlier. He had changed into a workman's shirt and denim pants which added to the lower-class appeal that many a rebellious young socialite—or perhaps their bored mothers?—would be drawn to for something sordid and noncommittal.

When he saw Penelope and Kitty there was no initial hint of recognition in his eyes. Still, he assessed them in an appreciative manner all the same, as though evaluating how likely it was either of them was there for something other than gardening work.

"Mr. Rizzo," Pen greeted. "I was hoping we could speak in private?"

"Sure," he said, a half-hitched smile coming to his face. He turned his attention to his uncle, brows raised as though asking for permission. His uncle waved a hand toward the back, a disgruntled look on his face.

Penelope and Kitty followed Salvatore through a set of doors that led to an outdoor patio filled with gardening supplies and tools. He turned around to face them, arms crossed over his chest and his tongue rolling around in his cheek once again.

"How can I help yous two?" he asked, sounding far different than he did back in the library. There was a hint of flirtation tinged with caution. He was probably wisely cognizant of the murder that had happened only hours beforehand.

"I'm Penelope Banks, and this is Kitty Andrews," she said. She dug into her purse and pulled out the gold lighter with a handkerchief. "I thought I should return this to you. I believe you may have dropped it underneath the sofa earlier today?"

"Huh," Kitty exhaled next to her, giving Penelope an annoyed look at not having been included in on this surprise.

Pen saved all her attention for Salvatore.

Instantly all hints of cockiness, flirtation, or amusement disappeared from his face. The tan coloring of his skin became paler as he put the lighter together with today's events in the courtyard, and categorized Penelope and Kitty accordingly.

"I don't know what you're talkin' about. I've never seen that thing before in my life."

"That's funny because both Kitty and I saw you use it in the courtyard when you lit Constance's cigarette? Ah well, perhaps the police would be interested in it. I'm sure someone recognizes it as belonging to Constance Gilmore. And a simple fingerprint comparison would identify—"

"Okay, okay!" He put his hands up defensively. "But it ain't what you think. I didn't kill her!"

"How did you come by this then?"

A defeated look came to his face and he sighed. "I swear it was nothing. Girls like that, they enjoy teasing a guy. I know it ain't goin' nowhere, but hey, it's a fun way to pass the time all the same, you know? Some rich girl who thinks the sun rises and sets to her pretty little—" He caught himself before stating something untoward.

He frowned and looked at the ground, taking a moment

before he composed himself again and gave them a direct look.

"It wasn't the first time Constance decided to have a bit of fun with me. But I never went further than she allowed," he insisted, one finger adamantly pointed toward them.

"And the lighter? The last I saw you two, she was putting it back into her purse."

His tongue rolled around in his cheek again and the cockiness came back. "We moved to a more *inconspicuous* location to, um, have a discussion. She gave it to me, told me she'd come by to get it after her stupid lunch was over. I wasn't about to say no thank you. You catch my meanin'?"

Yes, Penelope caught his meaning, all the more so since she knew full well just how far Constance was willing to go with a man. At least this one didn't seem to be otherwise spoken for.

"So you *did* expect something from her?" Kitty pressed.

He coughed out a cynical laugh and shook his head. "Listen, I ain't hurtin' for female attention. There's plenty a girls—and women," he added with a wink, "who could more than satisfy me. Constance was just...I dunno, a bit of fun. She wants to make Daddy mad or her guy jealous by playing with a guy like me, then I'm more than happy to accommodate."

"I get it," Penelope said before he expounded on that. She tilted her head to consider him. "You *were* aware she was engaged, no?"

He smirked and shrugged as though that wasn't much of a hindrance to him. "If anything, that made things less complicated. It wasn't like she was gonna leave him for me or anything."

"Was *he* aware of what she was up to with you?" Kitty asked.

He gave her a look as though to ask how he should know. "Wasn't my problem either way."

"But it could be if he found out. John Duke is an influential man, enough to cause problems for your uncle's business if he had a mind to," Penelope suggested.

A guarded look came to his face. "As far as I know, no, he didn't know, *capisce*?"

Penelope considered everything he had just told her. It wasn't suspicious, and as far as she could tell, he had no motive to kill Constance, at least not a glaring one. The only possibilities were, one, she hadn't allowed him to go as far as he would have liked and he got angry about it. In that case, taking the time to sneak into the room where the luncheon was being held and poison her drink didn't fit with a crime in the heat of passion.

The other possibility was that Constance, for whatever reason, may have threatened to tell her fiancé. Like Penelope had suggested, it would have the potential to destroy his uncle's business if John got it into his head to punish him over it.

But why would she have done such a thing? Based on what Penelope had seen between Constance and John, the two were a content enough couple, though appearances could be deceptive. Still, Constance had chosen her future father-in-law's home to champion this year. She may have been cunningly manipulative and mean-spirited, but she wasn't stupid. Why cause problems for herself by admitting to an affair with a gardener? Further, how would Salvatore have even known that she was planning to tell John Duke about her secret escapades in between duties as chair of the Young Ladies Historical Preservation Society?

"Well, I suppose that explains it," Penelope said with a sigh.

"Really?" Kitty asked, disappointed.

"Do *you* have any more questions?"

Kitty turned to him with a devilish grin. "How many other girls, er, *tease* you the way Constance did?"

He smirked. "Who says it's just girls?"

"I think that's enough," Penelope said. "This isn't for one of your columns, Kitty. Need I remind you of our priority?"

Kitty pouted but remained quiet.

"So, uh, are you going to tell the police about the lighter?" Salvatore asked, now understandably sporting a worried look. "You know what'll happen to a guy like me if you tell them about this. They'll use every reason to find me guilty and I'm done for."

He was right to a certain extent. Even the detective yesterday automatically cast a suspicious eye on him as soon as he guessed his heritage. Frankly, Penelope wouldn't have faulted Salvatore for not mentioning how well he knew Constance when he had been interviewed.

"No, I won't say anything—for now," she added in a warning tone.

He relaxed and gave her an appreciative smile.

"But...you said something about the lunch. Stupid. Was that your word or hers?"

He gave her a wary look, pausing before answering as though wondering if there was some catch. "Hers, I don't think she took the whole thing seriously. In fact, she kind of laughed when she talked about that house she was saving or whatever. Told me she only ran to be chair of the whole thing just to get back at some other girl and steal the wedding date."

"Marie Phillips?"

"Yeah, that's her name."

"Did she say anything more about the wedding dates?" Kitty asked, suddenly more curious.

His face wrinkled in confusion. "We didn't exactly waste time discussing weddings."

"Of course," Kitty said, disappointed.

"So, um..."

"You're secret is safe with us, again, *for now*," Pen repeated.

He nodded in resignation as though that was the best he could hope for.

Penelope and Kitty went back inside. His uncle stood up straighter again, the same apprehensive look on his face.

"Thank you for indulging me, Mr. Giordano, I assume?"

"*Si*, yes, Sal is my sister's boy. A good kid, although he does like to have a little bit too much fun at times," he said.

"So I've noticed," she said with a subtle smile.

"Don't worry, I think he's learned his lesson this time," Kitty said with a grin.

Once they were back outside Kitty started up with the questions. "What do you suppose he meant about Marie? What was Constance getting back at her for?"

"I should be asking you that. I'm surprised you don't already know."

Kitty bit her lip in thought. "I just assumed it really was all about winning the bet and being chairlady, but now I'm not so sure."

"Well, now we know she didn't even care about being chair, but she did care about the wedding date, presumably. But why turn it into a competition? What really started this war between them? Was it vicious enough to resort to murder?"

"And that outburst with the waiter? Maybe you and Jane had a point in retrospect. Who gets that upset over onions? It could have been an act of deception. That could very well have been when Marie put the poison in."

"Possibly, but we need a definitive motive first, which means learning the true cause of why Constance had such an ax to grind with Marie."

Kitty suddenly grinned. "I know exactly how we can find out."

"You do?"

"Yes, but I doubt you'll like it very much," she said with a sly look that Pen *didn't* like very much.

CHAPTER FOURTEEN

One didn't simply walk up to the residence of a family like the Phillips' and ring the doorbell. Despite being a member of the idle rich who commanded some form of advance notice on principle alone, they had full schedules of obligations to attend to. When your last name was on many of the buildings that patronized the arts, your social dance card was never empty.

Penelope knew that trying to call upon Marie was unlikely to prove fruitful. They weren't really friends and anyone who had any sense would know why she was interested in meeting with Marie.

In fact, Penelope would have hazarded a guess that a full team of attorneys had built up an impenetrable wall around Miss Phillips, one that a fellow suspect had no chance of breaching.

As such, she wasn't opposed to at least hearing Kitty out when she said she had an idea of how to learn more about Marie's feud with Constance. Desperate circumstances meant desperate measures.

They were in the car again with Leonard driving. Kitty apparently had no qualms talking in front of him.

"Think of it like one of those ploys that the police use to catch criminals. They announce that the criminal has won a prize and in order to collect, he—or she—must show up at a certain place at a certain time? This is no different. If Marie isn't guilty of anything, she has nothing to worry about."

Penelope already felt her stomach twist with uncertainty. "That sounds devious."

"Devious is my middle name. It's a messy business, Pen. Even you'll have to get your hands dirty at some point. You might as well get used to it with me. Or would you rather face arrest at the end of the week?"

That had Leonard turning quickly to give her a look of alarm.

She flashed a reassuring smile, then turned to Kitty, who had a point.

"I'm listening."

Kitty turned to Leonard instead. "We're going to the *New York Tattle* instead of Pen's office."

"Why there?"

"For this to work, this has to be completely plausible."

"Are you going to tell me what *this* is?"

"You'll see when we get there."

"Kitty..."

"No, this is what you get for keeping me in the dark about the lighter. I thought we were supposed to be partners. You surprised me, now I'm going to surprise you."

"If it's something that could get me into even more trouble..."

"Don't worry, your precious reputation will remain intact," she said with a taunting smirk, knowing full well that whatever reputation Pen had, it was already quite tarnished. "Besides, she could very well be Constance's killer. If she is, don't you want to use every avenue available?"

"Every *legal* avenue."

"It's legal," Kitty said, rolling her eyes and laughing.

Penelope sat back with a sigh. At the questioning look Leonard turned to give her, she nodded.

"I suppose we're headed to the *New York Tattle*."

The *New York Tattle* offices were still abuzz this late in the day. Apparently, there was a lot of mud to be slung in this city.

"It's an election year—for mayor—so the paper is especially busy these days. Rumor has it there might be an upset in the primaries."

Pen remembered voting for John Francis Hylan back in 1921, mostly out of obligation to the women who had fought so hard for her right to vote. He had seemed sensible enough at the time. She found the idea of politics quite boring and hadn't concerned herself with much of what was going on with the candidates this election year. Of course she'd vote—right after reading up on the important issues at the last minute.

None of which was a priority at the moment.

"We'll need to use the phone in these offices. Marie has to know that the extension is from the *New York Tattle*, just to make it seem more authentic. A call coming from the *Tattle* would cause the legs of most members of decent society to quake with worry before I've even said hello."

Penelope was fine with that. Whatever scheme Kitty was conjuring, she certainly didn't want the operator informing Marie or any of the other Phillips family members that the call was coming from her office.

"What exactly is it that is supposed to have Marie's legs atremble?"

Kitty grinned as she walked into an office that seemed to be dedicated solely to the phone. When she closed the door behind them, the noise of the open area beyond quieted to a hush and Penelope suddenly understood why.

"Watch and learn, Pen," Kitty said with a smug look as she picked up the receiver and placed it to her ear. She sat on the edge of the desk rather than the chair provided, then picked up the candlestick portion.

After connecting with the operator she asked to be connected with the Phillips residence.

Penelope watched with bated breath, wondering what she was going to say.

"Yes, can I please speak to Miss Marie Phillips?" Kitty finally said, staring off to the side with a lazy smile on her face. "This is Kitty Andrews from the *New York Tattle*. I strongly suggest she take this call, if only for her own good." She paused. "No, I think it's best I don't leave a message for privacy's sake."

Penelope's frown deepened. She wondered if Marie actually would come to the phone. So much time had elapsed since asking for her.

Kitty's eyes narrowed, telling Pen that Marie wasn't going to come to the phone. Still, the vicious smile that came to her face meant this wasn't exactly a problem.

"Fine then," she said curtly. "Please make sure and tell Miss Phillips word for word the following: I know exactly what happened during the argument with the waiter at the luncheon for the Young Ladies Historical Preservation Society. Furthermore, I know about the wedding wager she had with Miss Constance Gilmore and that there is more to it than everyone thinks. If she would like to avoid reading about it in the next edition of the *New York Tattle*, then it would be in her best interest to meet me at the Abercrombie Tea Room tomorrow at noon." She waited to make sure the person on the other end understood. "Yes, that is correct. Thank you, and please make sure that message is related to Miss Phillips as soon as possible."

Penelope's eyes went wide. She wasn't sure if she was shocked with horror or admiration. Perhaps a bit of both, though she was slightly ashamed about it. Still, as Kitty had pointed out, it wasn't illegal. The words were threatening enough, and if Marie had nothing to hide then she shouldn't have to worry.

Yes, the excuse sounded hollow in her own head, but then Pen reminded herself that, one, she was still very close to being arrested for a crime she hadn't committed, and two, Kitty wouldn't *really* print anything about Marie in the *Tattle*. This was all a ruse.

When Kitty hung up she was almost giddy. "Well, that was exciting. I do love a good bit of subterfuge. I feel like a spy during the Great War."

"You really are devious," Penelope observed.

"All for the greater good, Pen."

"I trust that means catching a murderer and not some sleazy tabloid article?"

Kitty smirked. "Of course. And if she happens to be the murderer, all the better."

Though she didn't share the enthusiasm of her "partner," Pen had to agree. Perhaps by noon tomorrow, they would have the identity of Constance's killer.

CHAPTER FIFTEEN

After Kitty's phone call, Penelope finally felt the weariness set in. Looking back on the day, it had been quite full, and quite the adventure. Certainly not a fun one. The murder itself, followed closely by the very real stress of her possible arrest, all combined with running across town chasing down clues had left her brain perfectly fried.

She knew it would be no use doing anything to pry information from either Alice or Eleanor, especially now that evening was setting in. After so many hours, the entire city would have heard about what had happened to Constance, and the wagons would be firmly circled. Pen would have to be just as creative and cunning (and most likely devious) as Kitty had been today in order to breach those forces. Right now, all she could get her mind to do was think about home and sleep, perhaps a nip of gin to help her along.

"Good evening Chives," she greeted when he opened the door for her. As he took her light coat she studied his stoically professional demeanor to try and determine whether or not Cousin Cordelia had heard the news yet.

Like any good butler, he could read her mind and quietly told her, "Mrs. Davies has been informed about the, ah, unfortunate incident. She's been in quite a state most of the day. She is currently in the living room with Lady Dinah. I would suggest something from the bar to prepare yourself."

She smiled tiredly. "Thank you, Chives. I assume she's already had her own dose of medicine?"

"Her medicinal brandy has made an appearance or two throughout the afternoon," he said diplomatically.

Pen laughed softly enough that no one would hear. "How has Jenny taken it?"

"Jenny has performed her duties as well as could be expected," he said, again diplomatically.

"I see," Pen said with a sigh. "Perhaps I should make a drink for her as well."

A subtle smile touched his lips as he put her coat away.

The layout of the apartment made it impossible for Pen to escape to her bedroom and change into something more comfortable without passing by the open living room. Fortunately, the bar was on the way. She poured herself a glass of gin and took a deep breath before heading to the living room.

"Good evening, Cousin Cordelia," she said in a light-hearted tone.

"*Murder?* Of all the things, Penelope!" Her cousin accused, giving her a look of supreme indignation.

"I see word has officially reached you."

Cousin Cordelia had Lady Di practically in a stranglehold, though the creature took it with her usual placidness. The kittens were wreaking havoc elsewhere in the apartment.

"Don't look at me that way. I certainly didn't kill her," Pen said, as she fell onto the couch next to her.

"Oh, Penelope, what am I to do with you?"

"Well, the police may solve that problem for you soon enough. It seems I am one of their main suspects."

"Oh, dear!"

The kittens suddenly made an appearance, the fully orange one leaping over to attack Pen's shoe. She picked him up with her free hand, mostly to keep his claws from destroying it.

"I'll bet you're glad I'm a private detective now, aren't you?" she said turning her attention back to her cousin as she scratched the tummy of the little ball of fur now lying on his back in her lap. At some point, they'd have to find homes for these three, or at least give them names. "I fully plan on solving this case and bringing the true culprit to justice."

She tried to sound more confident than she felt.

Right now it all looked fairly dire. Even if Marie did show up tomorrow, there was no assurance she would tell them anything. There was also no assurance that it would reveal her as the murderer.

"This is just too much," Cousin Cordelia cried, releasing Lady Di in favor of fanning herself. "Jenny!"

The new maid made an appearance, her brow already creased with exhaustion.

"My medicine if you will. You know where it is."

"Chives is perfectly capable of making you a proper drink," Penelope pointed out. "We practically have a full bar."

"I am not a *criminal*, Penelope," Cousin Cordelia hissed under her breath as Jenny escaped.

Penelope smiled to herself. Cousin Cordelia's "medicine" was nothing more than bootleg brandy. Any prescription she'd once had had expired years ago. Pen failed to see the difference between her medicine and any other illegally purchased alcohol, thanks to the horror that was Prohibition.

Jenny came back with the small glass flask that was refilled at least once every other week. She dutifully poured Cousin Cordelia a generous splash to calm her overly worked nerves. Then, she just as quickly exited.

"Do you want to hear about what happened?" Penelope inquired before taking a sip of her own "medicine."

"Of course not!" Cousin Cordelia scoffed. She frowned and considered Penelope under lowered lids. "But...if you feel you must talk with someone to lighten your burden, I suppose I could bear it."

Penelope bit back a smile. Of course Cousin Cordelia wanted to hear about it, as gruesome as it might be. She was always one for gossip and drama, and the death of a wealthy young socialite satisfied both wanton desires.

Pen started with Constance's appearance in the entryway and the fact that they were both surprised to see each other. From there she relayed everything, being perfectly tawdry about what had happened in the courtyard, much to Cousin Cordelia's delight. She was, however, far more delicate about the death itself, if only to protect her cousin's sensibilities, and perhaps Constance's dignity.

"The poor thing," Cousin Cordelia lamented. "I suppose it was fortunate her fiancé wasn't there to see it."

"Unless he was the one to poison her," Penelope said.

"What? He wouldn't, surely."

"Why not? A husband or wife is often the most likely suspect. Why not a fiancé?"

It was a consideration Pen hadn't completely dismissed herself.

"But certainly he loved her, no?"

"Love makes us do crazy things, Cousin."

"I refuse to believe it. What about this Kitty friend of yours? I've read her sordid little stories in the *New York Tattle*."

Of course she had, Penelope thought to herself.

"Who do you suspect may have done it?"

"Right now, I have no idea," Pen answered, taking a sip of gin. She considered her cousin over the rim, then swallowed. "You know, I never would have been there if Mrs. Winthorpe hadn't added me to the attendee list."

It took a moment for Cousin Cordelia to catch on. "I certainly hope you aren't insinuating that Tess had anything to do with this murder, nor her niece, Eleanor for that matter."

"I would never suspect such a thing," Penelope said adamantly enough to appease her cousin. "I'm just curious as to why it is Eleanor was so interested in my being there. The Society certainly doesn't need my money. Everyone there is worth more than I am, at least when it comes to family money."

"Have you considered that she was simply doing you a kindness? In the last three years, you've lost touch with many of your friends."

"Which is their failing, not mine," Penelope said, a little too bitterly.

"Now someone has graciously reached out the hand of friendship, and what do you do but swat it away. I swear this profession of yours has turned you into a perfect curmudgeon, Penelope."

Pen realized she would have to approach this in a different manner if she was to get answers.

"You're right, of course. Perhaps I should go to church with you this coming Sunday?"

"A splendid idea!"

"Do you usually sit near Mrs. Winthorpe? I'd very much like to thank her personally for taking the *liberty* of inviting me."

"Well...no. Naturally, the Winthorpes own a pew in the front."

"Naturally," Penelope said, keeping her cynicism to herself. The idea of the wealthy being able to purchase favorable seating in a church of all places had never agreed with her sense of Christian morality.

"And *she* was the one to approach *you* after service?"

"Yes," her cousin confirmed, beaming.

That irked Penelope even more. This interaction had obviously meant so much to her cousin, who was none the wiser that it had all been for some ulterior motive.

"Did she mention Eleanor at all? Specifically why she would want me to go to this meeting?"

"Aren't you pleased about that?"

"Of course," Penelope said quickly. "It's just, she *is* several years younger than me. We didn't really socialize when I was younger. I'm just curious as to why she's suddenly picked up the gauntlet in my honor."

"Perhaps she's taken pity on you? Now that she's a young woman, surely she can sense your need for female companions who are of the same social standing that you are?"

Penelope was hardly that credulous. The young woman she saw at today's luncheon seemed too standoffish to be that charitable.

"Though, Tess did mention Reginald, which I thought was odd."

"Really?" Penelope sat up straighter, surprised at the mention of her father's name.

"Perhaps she was unaware of the, er, current situation between you and your father. I certainly wasn't going to tell her, of course. Still, I was under the impression that it was well-known in most circles. I suppose that's why she had never before invited me to lunch, being that he cut me with the same swathe."

Yet another reason to despise Mrs. Winthorpe, obviously a snob who was only interested in someone when they were of value to her. Still, she wasn't about to ruin her cousin's tranquility with that notion.

"What did she say about my father?"

"She suggested that he might be interested to know that you were attending the luncheon."

Well, this was certainly odd. This whole time, she had been under the impression that Eleanor had been the main reason for her invitation to the luncheon; a notion that had made Pen more eager to question her before all the other candidates. Now, it seemed there was an altogether different reason.

One she still couldn't fathom.

"Why on earth would my father care about my attending the luncheon?" Penelope had to laugh at the idea.

"I know what it is!" Cousin Cordelia said, brightening up. "She thought he might be pleased to learn about you getting back into society. Surely that's it?"

"Right," Penelope said, taking a sip. She couldn't think of anything more wrong.

First of all, she doubted Mrs. Winthorpe was that

considerate of others' feelings. She had an agenda either of her own or as a representative of Eleanor. Secondly, Penelope's father didn't care one fig about her getting back into society. His only concern was that she didn't socially embarrass him.

Pen smiled at the idea that today would certainly cause him some heartburn. It was almost worth being a primary suspect if only to ruffle his stodgy old feathers.

The only other thing she could think of was that it was somehow related to the Duke House. But why would her father care about that? He was in finance, not real estate. He couldn't care less what went on in this city or its landscape so long as he made money. Perhaps there was some backroom dealing going on with the Dukes?

The only way to know for sure would be to talk to him. The idea of having any type of conversation with her estranged father reminded Penelope that there were other issues she needed to discuss with him, issues that had absolutely nothing to do with some silly house on Park Avenue.

Issues that had to do with her dearly departed mother.

Her last case had introduced Pen to some rather surprising information about her. As a child, Pen had been left mostly in the dark regarding her mother's past, knowing only that she was once a performer. The only person still alive who might know something about it was her father, with whom she was loath to so much as visit.

Now, it seemed she had reason to call on him.

But that was hardly a priority. It couldn't possibly be connected to Constance's death, which was just a wee bit more pressing right now.

She had a meeting with Marie tomorrow at noon. She had to find a way to meet with Alice and Eleanor as well, and she had no clue how to go about it. It was enough to have her bringing the glass of gin to her lips again to take a long swallow.

Even the detectives, as awful and bullheaded as they were, would have a difficult time wading through this world of money and power. They'd have to—

She sat up straighter as a thought occurred to her. "I've got it!"

"You've got what dear?" Cousin Cordelia asked with understandable alarm.

Penelope turned to smile at her. "A solution to an obstacle."

CHAPTER SIXTEEN

Pen woke up with the sun the next day and had Jenny set out her smartest outfit, one that oozed sophistication, and most importantly, money. She, more than most, should have realized how simple it was to ease one's way over hurdles when one was sitting on a pile of kale.

By ten o'clock, she was in one of the finer cars that Agnes had left her, with Leonard at the wheel of course. Appearance mattered more than anything this morning.

The New York First Bank had been established by some Todd family scion almost eighty years ago. The amusing, and very hush-hush tidbit was that it hadn't started in New York, and it certainly wasn't the first bank in the state. Still, it was one of the largest and most distinguished. There were rumors that the name would soon need to change to reflect its new status as it expanded into multiple states along the Eastern Coast, and eventually on to new horizons across the country and perhaps the world.

The interior of the bank was the sort of grand affair that gave prospective clients all the proper assurances that the men behind the scenes were flush with money. Every surface was marble or granite, perhaps even a tasteful touch of gold here and there. It also had the intended effect of making sure the average middle-income commoner knew this wasn't the bank for them.

Fortunately, Penelope had five million reasons for being a priority as a potential client, even for a last-minute appointment.

She wasn't surprised to see it was David Todd himself who came out to warmly greet her. The Todd family knew which of them would be their most successful ambassador, and he was the one to whom she had been closest.

"Miss Banks," he greeted with a gracious smile, not taking any chances on being overly familiar with her.

"Oh David, you know it's always been Pen," she said with a pleasant titter as he took her hand.

"Of course, Pen," he said with a bonhomie laugh. "It's so good to see you again."

"After so many years," she couldn't help but point out. None of the Todds had offered so much as a nod of acknowledgment after Pen had been cut off by her father. In fact, they had gone out of their way to side with Clifford in the hopes of securing business with the admittedly influential Stokes family.

"It has been a while. But you seem to have done well for yourself."

"Which is what brings me here," Penelope said, forcing herself to be gracious and polite, and most importantly, tactful. She wanted to make sure David saw her as an acquaintance as well as a client.

"Yes, of course," David said, his eyes lighting up with dollar signs. "You wish to open an account."

"I'm considering it," she hedged so there would be a reason to have an extended conversation.

"Let's go to my office where we can speak privately," he said, which was exactly what she'd been hoping for.

Penelope didn't feel at all guilty about this little bit of subterfuge, at least not this part of it. If Alice was innocent, Pen certainly had no intention of being malicious with whatever Constance had used to coerce her. If she turned out to be guilty, well, she would ultimately have to pay the price.

Back in David's office, he continued to treat her like an old friend who had come to visit. It was an act to lure her into business with the bank, but Penelope played along for her own purposes.

"I can have Martha my secretary get you some coffee or tea? Perhaps a lemonade?"

"No, I'm fine thank you," she said.

He gestured to his secretary and she obediently closed the door to give them some privacy.

"So, should I walk you through all the available options? We offer favorable rates above a certain deposit amount, many of which I think you'll find—"

"Oh David," she said with a pretty pout. "Let's not be so formal and business-like as that. I was hoping to at least catch up with you a bit, learn more about how you and the rest of the Todds are doing."

"Of course," he quickly said, mild panic hitting his eyes at the thought of losing her business. "I had been meaning to call on you at some point. You're back on 5th Avenue I heard?"

"Yes, in an apartment. I prefer it to the stuffy old mansion I grew up in." She quickly pivoted, not wanting to detour too far down the road of niceties. "But, I'm awfully concerned about Alice. After what happened to Constance Gilmore at the luncheon yesterday? I know how close she and Constance were. How is she, the poor dear?"

He blinked in confusion and mild irritation at the shift away from money. Then his gaze became guarded as he answered. "Fine, I suppose. I mean obviously it's a terrible thing. I understand you were there too?"

"I was, seated right at the table with Alice. It was awkward for me, as you might imagine, but I certainly wasn't expecting *murder*! I'm still shaken over it."

"Ah, y-yes," he stammered in agreement, now both embarrassed for Pen and guarded about Alice. "I suppose it must have been quite a shock."

"Alice and she must have been particularly close though. Why else would Constance have on Alice's pearl necklace?"

"I beg your pardon?" This was obviously a surprise to David, considering the look on his face. Any concern about Alice's potential culpability had vanished.

"The pink ones with an A on the clasp?"

"Those were our grandmother's pearls. She left them to Alice specifically because they both had names that started with A. Why on earth would Alice have given them to *Constance Gilmore*?"

"Oh, I thought you knew?" She planted a look of uncertainty on her face. "I do hope I haven't given away one of Alice's secrets. I suppose she had her reasons for giving such a beloved family heirloom to Constance."

David sighed and looked off to the side in anger, his jaw taut. "That damned, silly girl."

"Could she have been pressured or blackmailed or tricked in some way?"

He coughed out a laugh. "I wouldn't be surprised if she willingly gave them away."

Penelope certainly hadn't been expecting that. "Why would she do that?"

David seemed to suddenly remember where he was and sat up straighter, a curtain of professionalism masking his expression. "I shouldn't have said anything. This is hardly appropriate."

"Applesauce, we're friends, aren't we? I've always liked Alice. Like you, I only want what's best for her. If Constance manipulated her somehow—"

"Not Constance," he sighed looking off to the side.

Penelope's brow creased with uncertainty. "The man who helped work on your house?"

David's eyes snapped back to her, then a dark laugh escaped his lips. "I suppose I shouldn't be surprised that everyone knows about it by now."

Something about that tickled a thought in Penelope's brain, but she left it alone for now. "You think he may have persuaded her to give her pearls to Constance?"

David studied her, conflict coloring his eyes. Finally, he leaned in close enough to be confidential. "This boy, he's introduced her to a bad set, the kind of people who have put strange ideas into her head."

Penelope remembered Alice's outburst when the waiters seemed on the verge of a revolt yesterday. It had seemed a bit out of character for the girl she knew. Now, she had a better idea of it.

"Communists?"

David's eyes went wide with panic and he looked around, even though they were completely alone.

"David, there are certainly worse people she could be associating with, trust me," Pen said with a laugh, remembering some of the more unsavory characters with whom she had found herself entangled during the three years she illegally played cards for extra money. Poor Alice would be like a lamb among wolves with that set.

"This is hardly a laughing matter, Pen. The Todd family runs a bank, for heaven's sake. Can you imagine what would happen if word got out a member of our family was consorting with *communists*?"

Then what in the world was she doing at the Young Ladies Historical Preservation Society? Saving an abandoned mansion for the vainglorious pride of a wealthy family hardly aligned with ideals set forth in the *Communist Manifesto*, or at least what tidbits Penelope had learned about it. She had a preference for novels, mostly mysteries or romance, than economic-political treatises.

"Every young person goes through a period of rebellion, David. I seem to recall you weren't exactly a saint in your youth."

"That's hardly the same thing, Pen. It's one thing to move a professor's desk onto the roof as a prank, it's entirely different to align oneself with a group intent on destroying the very fabric of what holds decent society together! These people have no filter when it comes to association: immigrants, Irish, Italians, criminals, coloreds, libertines, Bohemians, orientals, even...*atheists*! You know I'm no segregationist, and I firmly believe that anyone should be able to come to this country and make something of themselves, so long as we aren't flooded with the wrong sorts. However, the people who bank with us aren't quite as *liberated* in their ways of thinking. They expect a certain level of—"

"Prejudice?"

Penelope was now reminded why their fleeting courtship had been rather lukewarm. As with many in the financial world—and bankers were certainly the stodgiest—

the Todds were insufferable bluenoses. No wonder even a duckling like Alice wanted to rebel.

Good for her.

"Yes, prejudice, at least in a manner of speaking," he conceded. "And it's perfectly understandable if you ask me. We aren't an investment bank, Pen, we're expected to keep our clients' money *safe* and *secure*. Now, my younger sister is gallivanting with people who believe all of it should be seized and divvied up among the lazy and the poor. She actually used the word feminist, the other day, can you believe that? What does that even mean? Nothing good, I'm sure."

"Don't you think you're being a bit overdramatic?"

"My concern is for her welfare, Pen. Father is threatening to cut her off, and she seems almost giddy at the prospect!"

Although Penelope fully applauded Alice's aplomb, she knew that the reality of such a drastic measure might prove more idealistic in theory than in reality.

"Why don't I talk to her? After all, I have some firsthand experience of having to fend for myself. I can paint a picture of what that life would really be like."

"Would you?"

"Of course."

Pen certainly had no intention of doing the Todd family's bidding, lassoing Alice back into the fold for the sake of their bank. Still, a dose of reality would help her make a more informed decision. Bully for her if she stuck to her guns.

More importantly, Pen planned on finding out what Alice's true motivations were. Why was she volunteering her services for a luncheon at which any true communist would have more likely staged a protest than attend? What was the real reason she had given Constance those pearls? What was her connection to that group of waiters?

Was it all some sinister plot to poison Constance?

Penelope left David Todd with the "promise to consider" depositing a substantial amount with their bank. He was understandably upset at not securing an account. Secretly, Pen wasn't quite sure that keeping her money "safe and secure" was worth it if it meant bolstering people with such a limited mindset.

As it stood, she *had* managed to secure an appointment to meet with Alice that very afternoon. If Marie actually showed up today at noon, it would be quite the busy day.

And hopefully an illuminating one.

CHAPTER SEVENTEEN

At noon, Penelope and Kitty were seated in a secluded corner of the Abercrombie Tea Room awaiting Marie Phillips's arrival. This particular tea room was a favorite for women who enjoyed a bit of gossip with friends. It offered several secluded seating areas to do just that while eating lunch and sipping tea.

Pen hadn't yet told Kitty what she had learned from David and was secretly devising a way to meet with Alice without her knowing. It wasn't so much that she didn't trust Kitty, though she didn't entirely, it was that Pen worried that both of them showing up to confront Alice might have her running scared, or going silent with fear.

"What do we do if Marie doesn't come?"

Penelope brought her mind back to the moment. "I suppose we'll cross that bridge when we—"

"She's here!"

Penelope flinched at Kitty's urgently whispered outburst. She darted her eyes toward the door where Marie had just entered. She was in pink today, a pretty straight-lined muslin dress. Kitty had a point about it being her color, whereas the buttercup yellow had given her a sickly pallor, the pink gave her complexion a youthful glow that made her look far more attractive.

She stopped short when she saw Penelope sitting with Kitty, who hadn't mentioned she would be there. Her gaze narrowed and Pen wondered if she would turn around and leave. Marie's eyes then landed on Kitty and turned to ice, but she continued walking toward them.

"Marie," Pen greeted neutrally.

Marie saved all her attention, heavily doused with venom, for the one sitting next to her.

"I don't know what you were insinuating with that phone call, Kitty. My parents already have an attorney on retainer to sue your paper into oblivion if you dare publish anything."

"I'm only in the habit of publishing facts, Marie. It *is* a fact that you got into a spat with the waiter right before Constance died from poisoning. And over something as petty as onions?"

Marie's eyes briefly flashed wide with alarm then cooled into something steely as she took a seat. "It was a minor disagreement over an entree. Yes, I may have overreacted but that's hardly newsworthy."

"It is if it was a distraction so that you could somehow slip poison into Constance's drink."

Marie stared at her for a moment, her face blank as though she was puzzling something out inside her head. Then she laughed. "Surely you aren't serious?"

"It's a perfectly plausible explanation for how it happened. And everyone knows you were bitter about the wedding date change as well as not becoming chair of the Society."

Again something flashed in her eyes before they

clouded over with derision. "I won't even threaten to sue over that one. Your publisher would have to be mentally insane to consider publishing something that false and defamatory. There is no crime in finding onions disgusting." She brought her hand up to her stomach as though it was turning at the prospect of eating them.

"*Was* there a wager involved with the election?" Penelope asked, switching to the other topic since Marie seemed intent on denying any subterfuge with regard to the waiter.

"The election?" Her eyes flashed to Penelope, wide with confusion.

"For the position as chair?"

She relaxed with comprehension and met Pen with the same cool gaze. "I won't bother denying it. Enough people have heard about it." She turned back to Kitty with a smug smile. "Go ahead and print it in your silly little gossip rag. Losing the position of chair is hardly worth killing over, nor is not having a spring wedding."

"Even after spending so much money on pink tulips?"

"Fortunately my parents can afford it. On the other hand, I *don't* think they'd appreciate me committing murder, do you?"

There was something they were missing, Pen could feel it. Why would Marie bother showing up simply to refute what everyone here seemed to know was true?

"What happened to make Constance decide to go to battle with you this way?"

Marie considered Pen with no hint of panic or alarm. Then she sighed with impatience. "It was over the box seats at the Phillips Opera House. The Gilmores had put in a petition to purchase one and were denied."

It was as petty as it was dire. While men may have concerned themselves with net worth and business ownership, their wives were far more concerned with society memberships and the perch from which they could view it all. Take for instance box seating at the best opera house in the city to gossip and spy on other members of high society. No one actually went to the opera just because they were an aficionado of Mozart's *Don Giovanni*.

"When she knew I was running for chairlady, I suppose that was her chance to get back at the Phillipses. To be fair, the denial was mostly because of Constance herself, and she probably knew that. She is—*was* a liability to her family. You aren't the only one she's wronged in the past," Marie said to Penelope.

Which made one wonder why the Dukes would have insisted on marriage.

"And why make the wager for the wedding?"

Marie threw up her hands in disbelief and anger. "As though I had a choice? Constance booked the Waldorf-Astoria. I was appalled when I found out. Everyone knew I had been planning a spring wedding for well over a year. We certainly couldn't have *two* society weddings this season!"

Once again Pen thought about how ridiculous that was, but she kept silent, being that Marie seemed ready to tell them everything.

"Then, like the conniving little shrew she is, she offered me the wager. It was either that or nothing. I thought victory was mine. I mean, who at the Young Ladies Historical Preservation Society would vote for Constance of all people? And...then she won somehow." Marie looked off to the side in wonder as though she was still left perfectly stunned.

A waitress came by to ask if they wanted to order something.

"Just a cup of tea for me, peppermint if you have it?" Marie requested.

Penelope ordered coffee and Kitty ordered oolong tea.

Marie found her composure as she continued. "So, as you can see there is no scandalous news, no delicious gossip, or tawdry secrets. A simple wager that's it."

Pen didn't feel that was it at all.

"Why did you want to be chair in the first place?" Penelope asked, mostly to make sure they explored every thread.

Marie narrowed her gaze with suspicion. "Why do you ask?"

"Surely there must be a reason?" Penelope asked, feeling that she was on to something.

"It's an important position, one of the few for young women like me that might actually accomplish something."

"What building would have been your focus had you won?"

Marie twisted her lips. "Certainly not some pointless relic like the Duke House which is really nothing more than a ploy, let's face it." She coughed out a laugh. "Samuel Duke's pride won't allow him to let go of it, even as skyscrapers are going up all around it. It's a complete farce, one that is only stalling progress. I would have focused my efforts on Trinity Church, which is in need of repairs and is actually something worth saving. Alexander Hamilton is buried there."

The tea came back on the heels of that and Marie instantly took a sip of hers, humming in appreciation. She set it down and focused her attention back on them. Her nose wrinkled as she looked at Kitty, now sipping her own tea.

"Goodness, did you have to order something so

pungent, Kitty?" She asked, her hand coming to her nose. Her face went pale, then almost green with disgust.

It triggered something for Pen, a chapter she'd read in a book she was far too young to have read at the time. Something she recalled now, word for disturbing word. Something that had solidified her hesitation to ever....

"Oh my God, you're—!" she stopped herself before blurting out the words. Instead, she leaned in to give Marie a pointed look.

Now Marie was perfectly ashen, looking as though she would once again expel the contents of her stomach.

"What?" Kitty asked, sensing something important pass between them. "What is it?"

"None of your business," Marie snapped.

"If Constance knew, it would definitely be a motive for murder," Pen said. "She *did* know, didn't she?"

"She didn't know," Marie said a little too defensively.

It all made sense now, the coded language Constance had used: *Marie, you are looking a bit green. Is there something weighing on you?*

Marie's glow wasn't from wearing her favorite color. The nausea, the disdain for odors like onions and oolong tea, the looser dresses.

Definitely a motive for murder.

"Okay fine," Marie said, sitting up straighter and steeling her gaze. "Yes, I am with child."

Kitty gasped with delight. Pen exhaled the breath she'd held.

But Marie looked a little too smug.

"Go ahead and print it, Kitty. It doesn't matter—because I'm already married."

"What?" Penelope asked in surprise.

Marie gave her a cool smile. "When I lost the election

and I realized I wasn't going to have my spring wedding. Brandon and I eloped." She turned to Kitty. "We have the marriage license to prove it."

She settled back in her seat, for once relaxed, as though she'd been carrying that secret around as a burden. "Honestly, I'm glad it's out. We were going to announce soon anyway. You've given us the perfect excuse."

"But, why keep it a secret in the first place?" Pen asked.

Marie's mouth tightened with something approaching anger and she took a moment to sip her tea, savoring it.

"There must be a reason," Kitty said in a voice that grasped on to one final thread of hope for something worth writing about.

A look of resentment flashed across Marie's face, which Pen assumed was for Kitty's doggedness. She set her tea down and met both of them with a hard look that had them paying closer attention.

"If you report this, I will make it my personal mission to destroy you, and not just the paper you work for," she began, then waited for some hint of acknowledgment from them. Both Kitty and Pen nodded. "My sister, she...they haven't been blessed yet, despite being married for nearly two years now. The thought was that..." she paused and the resentment came back to her face.

"Was that they would simply claim your baby as theirs," Penelope said quietly.

She had seen it done before. A young girl took an extended vacation for unknown reasons. In this case, perhaps Marie and her sister would go off together, but the older one would be happily blessed with a new baby when they returned. There would, of course, be murmurs but rarely did people openly make accusations.

Marie nodded and sipped her tea, it seemed to ease some of the anger in her.

"I do love my sister, and I certainly sympathize. She's always wanted children. But this one here," Marie cradled her stomach. "I tried to think of it as not mine, that it wouldn't be so bad to be in his or her life as an aunt, but I couldn't."

"But you were married, there was no need for that cover," Kitty pointed out.

"My parents care about appearances. An elopement conjures up all kinds of unsavory ideas. Better to do things the right way, including the society wedding. After all, it wasn't as though I couldn't have more children, seeing as how easily it happened for me. And Louise's husband *needed* an heir." She glowered with resentment.

Kitty and Penelope were silent as she took another sip, then brightened back up with a smile.

"But, happily, it has proven unnecessary. It seems my sister will also be blessed. Obviously, my parents aren't happy about the elopement. They would rather do things the traditional way. But this is a new era, if I can't have my pink tulips then I see no need for a full-blown wedding." She gave Kitty a hard look. "And just in case you intend to make spurious suggestions, the due date is well within the bounds of legitimacy."

Now when she picked up her tea to sip, there was an ease and lightness to her that told Penelope that was all she had to give.

"This was all settled long before yesterday's luncheon. My parents wanted to wait as long as possible just in case, but my sister has started showing by now so it's pointless to withhold the truth." Her mouth curled as she addressed Penelope. "So you see, I had no reason to kill Constance. I may have been upset about the wedding and losing position of chair but in the end, I've gotten everything I really wanted."

"Except perhaps saving Trinity Church," Penelope offered.

"Yes, I suppose there's that," she said in a slightly sardonic tone. No one at the table considered that a motive for murder.

She finished the last of her tea and rose from her seat. "I would wish you a good day, but to be honest, I'm not feeling all that magnanimous."

Marie turned on her heels and walked out.

Kitty and Penelope watched her go, both feeling stunned and defeated.

"What now?" Kitty asked.

Now, Pen would have to move on to Alice. However, she needed an excuse to give Kitty.

"I think maybe the Duke House might have something to do with all of this. As you said, Park Avenue is quite popular these days for development. Perhaps you could see if there's something there."

"You don't think the Dukes had anything to do with the murder, do you?" Kitty looked perfectly incredulous.

"No, but maybe someone isn't happy about them trying to protect their mansion. Maybe they took it out on Constance?"

Kitty considered that idea with less reluctance.

Now that Pen had said it, it wasn't a bad idea. Money was just as much a motive for murder as hatred was.

"Perhaps the *New York Tattle* has some archives or recent stories on the topic?"

"The *Tattle* doesn't really write about business or real estate, not unless there's corruption involved—or enough money to cause the public to pick up the pitchforks." She studied Pen, eyes slightly narrowed. "What are you going to do?"

"I have to speak with my father."

Not an untrue statement even if it wasn't her first order of business. "I might need his advice in seeking counsel should I end up getting arrested."

That was enough to appease Kitty's suspicions and she nodded. "On to the next lead it is, I suppose."

CHAPTER EIGHTEEN

Penelope had decided to meet Alice in Central Park, which would give them as much privacy as anywhere else. It was March and the weather was pleasant enough to make a nice stroll of it. She sat down to wait on a bench near Grand Army Plaza, which was a recognizable landmark.

When Alice made an appearance, Pen could see the apprehension and determination on her face. She wasn't quite the timid girl who had greeted her when she first entered the Peyton Foundation House. There was something different about her.

"I know why my brother wanted me to talk to you, but it's pointless. I love Liam, I really do. I don't care that he's poor and has ideas that my family abhors, he has plans that I admire."

She said it with enough vehemence to have people nearby turning to stare with interest.

"Let's go for a walk," Penelope said gently, rising from the bench to hook her arm through Alice's.

"If you're here to talk me out of it then—"

"That's not why I'm here, Alice. I understand what love can do to you, how it can make you feel."

And how! Penelope thought. She hoped for Alice's sake, Liam was worth it, unlike Clifford was for her.

"Then why are you here?"

Penelope paused, wondering how to gently extract the information she needed. She decided to be upfront. After all, Alice was an adult. "I noticed Constance wearing your pearl necklace yesterday. Did you give it to her?"

Alice was silent for a moment, staring ahead at the winding path they were now aimlessly following.

"I did," she said quietly.

"Why? David said your grandmother left them to you. I assume they were special?"

Alice nodded and sniffed. She quickly composed herself and inhaled, standing a little more erect as she turned to face Penelope.

"It doesn't matter, pearls are worthless trinkets. Nothing more than baubles for the elite class to flaunt and—"

"Alice, just because you're a communist doesn't mean you have to give up personal mementos that hold special meaning for you."

Alice blinked in surprise. "David told you I was a communist?"

"I guessed as much."

"It's nothing to be ashamed of," she said defiantly. "It's a worthy aspiration for society. The schism between the bourgeoisie and the proletariat in this city is criminal. It should have everyone protesting in the streets at the injustice of it all."

"I agree," she said causing Alice to blink in surprise. Yes, Penelope certainly enjoyed living a luxurious life. That didn't mean she didn't think more should be done to lift everyone to a decent standard of living.

Pen tilted her head to consider Alice. "Were you and the waiters planning something like that yesterday?"

Alice's face went violently red, and Penelope knew she had been right about this suspicion of hers.

"We didn't kill Constance, I swear!"

"What did you have planned?" It wasn't beyond thinking that perhaps the waiters had different ideas than Alice did when this plot was first put together.

"Once the meals were served, the plan was to stage a protest. Everyone would be seated and it would be a sort of captive audience. Wyatt had a speech prepared and everything. That's why I was there organizing everything. I was the one to get them hired in the first place. But...then Constance died and it all just..." Alice broke down, tears erupting.

Penelope put her arm around her to console the poor girl. If she was putting on an act, it was a good one. From what she remembered Alice was incredibly guileless, and she doubted even the influence of a communist boyfriend could change her personality that much.

It certainly looked like Alice wasn't the culprit for Constance's murder. But that didn't mean she hadn't been used in some malicious way.

When Alice had finally settled, pulling away and wiping the tears from her eyes, Penelope cautiously pressed on.

"Is it possible that Wyatt didn't think a protest would be enough? Maybe he thought it would make more of a statement to kill Constance?"

Alice furiously shook her head and a determined look came to her face. "There's a strict non-violence rule in place. We don't want to be mistaken for anarchists, Penelope. We're not murderers, despite what certain individuals and groups would have you think. I mean, yes, the Tsar and his family were a tragic event, but that was the Bolsheviks, not us. Communism is peaceful, we believe in equality for everyone. Murder serves no purpose other than to make it more difficult for us to accomplish our goals. It paints us as villains when really we're heroes."

At the very least the movement had an ardent supporter in Alice. This conversation was proving to be unfruitful.

"Why did you really give Constance your pearls? I can see possibly not wearing them anymore, maybe even selling them for your cause. But giving them to *Constance*?"

Alice went silent, and Penelope got them walking again, waiting for her to open up. She sensed this might be a possible lead.

She heard Alice exhale next to her.

"You know what? It doesn't matter anymore what Constance knew. What she threatened to..." Alice stopped again and turned to Penelope with fire in her eyes. "Constance knew what was going on at the bank, my family's bank."

Penelope's eyes widened in surprise. She glanced around wondering if anyone could hear them. There was no one within hearing distance, but they were on a path and the weather was pleasant enough for anyone to wander by at any moment to enjoy the park.

"What was going on at the bank?"

"Bribery and corruption." Alice spat with a laugh. "I don't think there's a highbender in this city whose hand my family hasn't greased."

Pen's brow rose at the slang coming from her mouth

with regard to a dishonest politician. Alice really was getting an education.

"It's an election year so money is flowing like slime, oozing over every seedy part of this city. Something major is happening and New York First Bank is right at the corrupt center of it all!"

"I see," Penelope said, her heart quickening as she urged Alice along to a more remote area off the path. Her voice had been steadily rising, such that passers-by were turning to look. The last thing Pen wanted to do was add another scandal to this mess.

"The utter hypocrisy of it all," Alice continued undaunted. "And *I'm* the black sheep of the family? *I'm* the one who is immoral?" She coughed out a bitter laugh.

"So Constance came to you with this information and—"

Alice shook her head again. "No, no. I already knew. My family, they treat me like I'm not even there sometimes, like I'm nothing more than a doll in the background to be pampered and petted and pushed and pulled this way and that. At least until Liam and I..." She blushed and looked at Penelope under lowered lids. "He's the one who opened my eyes, made me feel like a person in my own right. Of course they ruined him for it. Little do they know that he was the one to suggest that I think long and hard before telling anyone. He knew it would damage them, maybe even ruin them, and he didn't want that guilt on my shoulders. And they think he's so terrible; if they only knew!"

At least he seemed like a decent man, unless he had some other motive for keeping it private. But she was more focused on the first part of Alice's statement.

"So Constance blackmailed you with this information?"

"Yes, and I suppose I was so worried about it I just gave

in. Liam is right, they are still my family after all, and I knew how terrible she could be about things. So when she demanded the pearls, I gave them to her." She lifted her chin and her gaze sharpened. "But that's why I wore the matching earrings yesterday. It was an act of defiance. The thing about Constance is, she doesn't just take, she likes to tease you after the fact. If I ever wore the earrings, she'd threaten to tell everyone my secret until I stopped wearing them. She did that to everyone. Why do you think Marie stopped wearing pink around her? And Eleanor with that scarf John gave her. There was something going on between Constance and Kitty too, but I'm not sure what. I knew yesterday it wouldn't matter anymore. Wearing those earrings was my one act of defiance, a signal to her that her control over me was at an end. After Wyatt's speech, I planned on demanding that she give back the necklace, that I no longer cared what she said about the bank. If they're doing something wrong, the world has a right to know, even if it comes from her."

"How did she know about it? Did she say?"

Alice shook her head. "She never said, and I have no idea."

"And you don't know exactly where all this money is going? You mentioned something major happening, do you know what it is?"

Alice sagged and gave her an apologetic smile. "No, I suppose my family isn't *that* negligent. But whatever it is, obviously involves money and a lot of it."

"What doesn't?" Penelope said.

They both snorted at that.

"You wouldn't happen to know of any reason why someone would want to kill Constance, would you?"

"Well, she wasn't very popular," Alice said sheepishly.

"An understatement." Indeed it was, which did nothing to help Penelope.

Pen guided them back to the path to continue walking, arm in arm.

"So you really plan on giving all of this up for Liam?"

"I have no doubts," Alice said without hesitation. A smile formed on her face. "I know it will be different, difficult even. Communists aren't popular, but...I just feel so, I don't know, good? I feel like I'm actually contributing something. As a Todd, a female one at that, I felt nothing. Like my whole life was planned out for me, a series of luncheons and parties and dresses and...it's all so pointless."

Pen certainly wasn't going to be the one to talk her out of it if she was that passionate. She was an adult.

"Do you think I'll be able to get the pearls back?" Alice asked nibbling her bottom lip.

Penelope patted Alice's hand reassuringly. "I'm friendly with a detective who can certainly see that whatever pearls were collected at the scene are returned to you."

"Thank you, Pen."

"You're welcome, and I truly do wish you good luck with all of this, Alice."

"I suppose you'll need it as well. It seemed as though that detective already considered you a primary suspect before I even opened my mouth, what with your experience and all."

"Of course he did," Penelope said with a sigh.

Alice was right, she was going to need some luck to come her way. And soon.

CHAPTER NINETEEN

Penelope had dropped by the office and asked Jane to go to the library and look into the newspaper archives for the past year and gather anything related to politics, particularly any major issues that might be of special concern this election year.

Now, she was headed home to get a strong glass of gin and devise an even stronger plan of attack for the final few suspects she had left to go through before she was arrested. Alice and Marie presumably no longer had secrets for Constance to hold against them. She still wasn't sure what Eleanor's was, and she hadn't written off John Duke.

Nor Kitty Andrews, for that matter.

But it was now dusk, and she wanted to nap some, then maybe organize her thoughts later in the night. Sometimes that worked well for her.

"Good evening, Chives," she greeted her butler as he met her at the door.

"Good evening, Miss Banks. You have a visitor."

"I do?" she asked in alarm, concerned it was the detectives who had come to finally make an arrest. "Who is it?"

"A Miss Eleanor Winthorpe. She's in the living room with Mrs. Davies."

"Eleanor Winthorpe?"

Well, that certainly solved one problem.

Still, Pen didn't like the idea of her arriving unannounced. It felt too much like an ambush. She went into the living room to confront Eleanor, who was indeed sitting with Cousin Cordelia. She was idly sipping coffee as Pen's cousin chattered away.

"Isn't this nice, Penelope?" Cousin Cordelia said, noting Pen's arrival. She gave her an encouraging smile. "Miss Winthorpe has come to call on you. How very kind."

"Eleanor," Penelope said cordially. "To what do I owe the pleasure of a visit?"

Eleanor lowered her cup of coffee and subtly lifted one eyebrow. "I thought we should have a talk in private."

"I think that would be a fine idea. Perhaps the library?"

Eleanor gave a barely perceptible nod and rose. She graciously thanked Cousin Cordelia, who positively glowed in response.

Once they were in the library, doors firmly closed, all pretense was shed, at least on Penelope's end.

"Why don't you tell me why it is you're really here? Furthermore, explain why it is you invited me to the luncheon in the first place. Was it to frame me for this murder?"

Eleanor didn't respond right away. Instead, she casually walked over to the windows and looked out over Central Park. She noted the stained glass doors bordering them, ones similar to those in the Peyton Foundation House. The fingers of her left hand idly traced along the lines and petals of the flowers before coming to rest against the green glass bordering them.

"My mother would love these. René Gauthier, no? It's so difficult to find authentic pieces anymore...and these are all yours."

Penelope exhaled with exasperation. "I'm so glad you like them?" She said in an expectant voice, encouraging Eleanor to get to the point.

Eleanor spun around to face Penelope.

"It's wonderful to have things of your own, isn't it? To not have to play nicely and be a good little girl, put on a stoic facade in public even when acid tongues long to wag about you." She waved her hand around the room. "You're lucky to have all of this, completely on your own without any burdens, save perhaps taking in your older cousin."

"I hardly consider her a burden," Penelope said. "And you haven't answered the question."

Eleanor's gaze suddenly steeled. "I thought I would save you the trouble of hunting me down to publicly humiliate me, the way you seem to have done with everyone else so far."

"My intent isn't to humiliate but to get at the truth. Which has me repeating the question of why—"

"Okay, yes, the truth is I invited you in order to humiliate Constance. It's as plain as that," she said, exhaling with finality. "I wanted to see the look on her face when *she* was the one stunned with embarrassment. Everyone knows what happened between you and her and Clifford Stokes."

"Is this because John was once your fiancé?"

Eleanor nodded.

"I was under the impression things had ended amicably between you two?"

"No one knows the real reason I broke it off with him, except Constance of course. The truth is, the same thing happened to me that rumors tell me happened to you. I caught her with him." Eleanor's eyes fell and she took a deep breath before coughing out a humorless laugh. "It was on my twenty-first birthday of all days, right in my own home last spring. A moment that should have been in my honor, tainted by...the two of them kissing."

"She does know when to pick her days, doesn't she?"

Eleanor flashed a tight smile. "No, I suppose it's not as bad as the day before one's wedding, but it stung all the same."

"Of course," Penelope said sympathetically. She paused, giving the moment the proper amount of gravitas, before continuing.

"I still wonder why it is you pointed the finger at me with Detective Beaks. He was the detective who spoke with you first, then Salvatore, the gardener, who wouldn't have known anything about my past. Alice claims that he already knew by the time he got to her. So...why?"

"He was the one to ask me if anyone else had a motive or opportunity. What was I to do? Pretend I didn't know about your history with Constance? I was trying to save my own neck as well, Penelope. After all, I certainly didn't kill her. He would have found out eventually. Much like my history with her fiancé, yours isn't much of a secret. I certainly never claimed you did it, in fact, I made mention of the fact that you were sitting furthest from her at the table."

"But there were the few minutes I was gone. And he knew about my past cases, one involving poison."

"I never told him that much," she said, giving Penelope a look of incredulity. "I wouldn't have gone *that* far to take the focus from myself."

Then how did he know?

"There's also the matter of your secret."

"Which I just told you..." Eleanor said, suddenly guarded.

"I don't mean the one about John and Constance, I'm referring to the real secret, the one only she knew about."

Eleanor was silent, her face unreadable. "What do you mean?"

"I mean, finding John kissing Constance is certainly painful and embarrassing, but not necessarily a ruinous or well-kept secret. No one has any proof in either case, but the rumors have certainly circulated. So, what is it Constance really had on you?"

"I don't know what it is you think you know," she said, her breath coming in heavier.

"I know that there are very poorly kept secrets floating around, minor embarrassments at best, barely enough to warrant a mention in the *New York Tattle*. I also know there are deeper secrets that certain young ladies would be horrified to ever have come to light. The kind of secrets Constance used as leverage and enjoyed not so subtly reminding people about, say by wearing a scarf almost identical to the target of her taunting?"

For a moment, Eleanor remained stoic, then a slow, sad smile spread her lips. "I can see why you've chosen to become a private detective. I'd heard of your strange ability to remember everything, but you seem to be rather perceptive as well."

"I'd like to think so."

"Very well," Eleanor said sighing and wandering the library her gaze passing over the many different titles rather than facing Penelope. She finally came to a stop, took a deep breath, and turned around to face Pen. For a moment she just stared, worrying her inner cheek with her teeth.

"If I tell you, will you promise to keep it confidential?"

"I have no reason to tell anyone your secrets," Penelope said, which wasn't exactly a promise to stay quiet. If the secret turned out to be evidence of a motive, combined with more solid proof of murder, she had no qualms about telling.

"When I was much younger I was far less reserved than the woman you see now. It was that period when cars were becoming more popular, and I was fascinated by them. I couldn't wait to drive one of my own. Of course my family instantly forbade it. Cars were not meant for proper girls, especially not a Winthorpe. But I couldn't let it go.

"I secretly paid one of the chauffeurs from another family to teach me how to drive, and I loved every moment of it. The only problem was the lack of access to a car. So, one night I..." She paused, looking away and swallowing hard. " I foolishly stole his car, or rather the one he drove for the family that hired him. It was so late and so dark, I fell asleep behind the wheel and crashed into a tree."

She sighed and her brow wrinkled with regret as though remembering it all over again.

"It didn't take long to discover that he'd been the one teaching me how to drive. Other more spurious accusations were thrown about, despite my protest that nothing of the sort took place." Her eyes finally met Penelope's. "You can imagine what happened to him. He was left without a cent. No family would hire him after that. It was all hushed up, and the family appeased—the double-edged sword of money and threats. What newspaper in New York would publish the story? We owned most of them. The *New York Tattle* didn't even exist then.

"Still, I had ruined a man's livelihood for a stupid lark. I tried paying what I could, selling some of my jewelry and such. At least until my parents found out and put a stop to it.

"As for the chauffeur, well, he took the only job he could get, illegally running alcohol from Canada across the border. A dangerous profession of course, and the last I'd heard of him, he'd been shot and killed.

"I've tried to atone for my sins. I behave as I should, say the right things, or better yet, nothing at all. Even my emotions I've managed to keep bottled up, for fear of giving too much away. I surround myself with the proper sort of female companionship so my family has the connections it needs. We're fairly new money, which puts an extra burden on us not to have any scandal. Honestly, even though I've never been to prison, I still feel like I've lived in a self-imposed one ever since."

"Now you know what Constance had on me," she looked past Penelope's shoulder in thought. "The funny thing is, in retrospect, I was grateful for Constance. Much like you should be, Penelope. Any man who is that easily led astray is certainly no one worth marrying."

"That's an awfully generous outlook to have on the matter."

Her eyes came back to Penelope.

"Being generous has nothing to do with it. I realized that I never really wanted to be married. It's just another prison to be constrained by. It took losing the man I almost married to learn this about myself."

Her eyes suddenly blazed with excitement.

"I plan on making my own way in the world, living a life of adventure as an independent woman, and I have every intention of making that happen. Do you know Nellie Bly? The woman who actually did travel the world in less than eighty days?"

"Of course." Nellie Bly was a journalist who Pen's mother had invited to one of her infamous dinners. Her life's adventures had held everyone else at the table captive. Pen had been saddened to hear of her death three years ago.

"That's who I'd like to become. I want to travel around the world on my own, explore uncharted territory, break records, sail the seven seas, fly in hot air balloons. I already have my New York pilot's license, unbeknownst to my family. There's a woman named Amelia Earhart who has broken a record for female pilots, flying higher than 14,000 feet in the air. Alone! Can you imagine? I want to go higher, much higher. Surely you of all people can appreciate being that wild and free, Penelope, defying what society expects of you?"

The way Eleanor spoke, showing the first signs of vivacity and passion about something, it transformed her from beautiful to stunning. Her fervor was contagious. It made Penelope want to live life even more boldly than she had been. Suddenly she imagined flying planes or maybe traveling to the bottom of the ocean or even the center of the Earth, the other adventures that Jules Verne had imagined.

"I'm only twenty-one and my mother already had my future plotted out for me, marrying someone just like John Duke, wasting my days away at luncheons like the one we attended, having children, raising girls who will probably be afforded more opportunities in life than I ever was, at least with any luck. My father only cares that the match serves his business interests. Neither of them cares about what I want."

This was another area where Penelope could relate, and in fact, sympathize. It also made her think of something else she meant to ask Eleanor.

"What does my father have to do with this? Why would you care that he knew I was attending the luncheon?"

Eleanor blinked at the shift in topic.

"That was my aunt's doing. She and my uncle had an entirely different motive for wanting someone like you there and telling your father about it. I confess I used it to my advantage. But as far as what they wanted?" She smiled encouragingly. "What do you suppose it is about him that might invite such interest?"

Penelope breathed out a laugh of impatience. "You're apparently unfamiliar with just how estranged I am from my father. In fact, I make it a point to think about him as little as necessary. So perhaps you can fill in that void for me?"

"He's an alderman, fourteenth district."

"Is he?"

The title meant very little to Penelope. Zounds, she'd really have to start developing an interest in politics. It would be a priority once this nonsense was over.

To her, the Board of Aldermen had always been an amorphous group that wielded a certain degree of power over New York City. During the last election, she hadn't even picked a candidate for that position in her district, not wanting to inadvertently be responsible for choosing someone horrible. But she certainly would have remembered Reginald Banks being one of those candidates. Then again, Pen and her father had lived in entirely different districts the last time she'd voted.

"If they thought my attendance would make it seem like I was making amends with Constance, they would have been sorely mistaken. Even my father isn't that gullible."

"I suppose I'll have to relay that message to them.

Though, I suppose at this point her murder makes everything moot."

"Because the Duke House is once again vulnerable?"

"Exactly," Eleanor said. "You've been focusing on silly secrets and scandals when this may very well boil down to politics and money."

"What would killing Constance accomplish?"

"Perhaps we young ladies weren't the only ones she was blackmailing? As you know, she liked to take things and lord them over her victims. Perhaps the Duke House was yet another example? The Dukes didn't look all that happy to be there at the luncheon in support of their own house, did they? One might wonder if there was trouble brewing before the nuptials even took place. What is it Constance was threatening them about?"

Pen considered that.

"Either way, I didn't like Constance, but I certainly didn't kill her. Yes, with her gone, my secret is safe. I hope I can trust you more than I did her?"

"I'm not Constance, I have no interest in making your life miserable with this."

"Thank you," she said, showing a bit of emotion yet again with her earnest relief and appreciation. "I suppose I'll give you back your evening. Good night, Penelope."

Pen said goodbye but remained in the library with a frown on her face considering this new avenue of investigation.

Why would anyone care about the Dukes' house? Politics? Money? Pride?

Perhaps all three.

Which meant moving the Dukes to the top of her list.

CHAPTER TWENTY

THE NEXT MORNING BACK AT THE OFFICE, THE CHAOS began early on. Jane was already in, as usual, by the time Penelope arrived.

"Did you find anything interesting at the library?"

"Well, this election is certainly going to be a humdinger," she said with bright eyes. "This man running for mayor, Mickey Driver? He's up against the current mayor as the democratic candidate and there may be an upset in the primary, maybe even the whole election. To top it off, Mr. Driver has a habit of spending a little too much time with chorus girls, and he frequents *speakeasies!*"

"Really?" Penelope said, already liking him.

"Those are just the scandalous bits."

"What about the issues he's campaigning on?"

"He's made a lot of promises, which has made him quite popular. There are a lot of social welfare programs he wants to enact, and he's publicly condemned the Ku Klux Klan. Even I think both of those are swell."

"So do I, though I imagine there are some who don't." Penelope doubted the Todds' bank money went to this

Mickey Driver if this was where he stood on the issues. "Anything else?"

"Let's see, he wants to legalize boxing again. I can't say I agree with that. And he wants to repeal the, um, blue laws? The ones that prevent baseball games on Sunday." She checked her notes again. "Oh, he's also promised to get rid of trolleys, I suppose to make way for more cars on the roads. None of the other candidates, even the current mayor have been willing to go that far on the issue."

"Really," Penelope said perking up. "Now that is interesting."

A major part of the Dukes' railway empire included trolley cars. Anyone who owned a trolley car company would be opposed to this Mickey Driver winning. On the other hand, those who had put their money into automobiles would be glad of it.

The only possible relation to this case that Penelope could see was that there was a trolley line that ran down 4th Avenue, which is what Park Avenue turned into south of 34th Street. But the Duke House was just north of that, so why would they care?

Perhaps Kitty might have dug up something about it.

"Good job, Jane."

Before she could compliment her further, Kitty burst in like a firecracker.

"It's all about Park Avenue!" she practically yelled, her face lit up with excitement.

Penelope felt her heart quicken. Perhaps this was coming together after all, a new motive. With Eleanor's suggestion last night, Jane's research into the election, and now this, perhaps she *had* been looking in the wrong place this whole time. She should have been focused on the Duke House all along.

"What have you found?"

"It's a big hullabaloo with a company called Park Avenue First owned by some egg named Fredrick Carpenter. He's a new real estate developer that's been buying up properties left and right and turning them into apartment buildings. He obviously has his sights set on Park Avenue, what with it being the sizzling address to be at these days. But that's just where it starts. You see—"

Before she could continue, another whirlwind of a personality blew in.

"How could you be involved in another murder case —*the* murder case of the *decade*, mind you—and not tell your best friend in the world?"

"Benny," Penelope said, already feeling her exasperation set in. She should have known Benny Davenport would have the news by now.

Yes, he was a friend, and to be fair, he had played a major role helping in her prior cases. Still, Benny lived for sordid gossip and fun more than anything. Two things she didn't exactly need right now.

"And *Kitty*?" He stared at Kitty, aghast, then turned to give Pen a look of utter disdain." If you're interested in scraping the bottom of the barrel, Pen, I'm sure I could scour up a more impressive bit of moldy crumb."

"And if she needs to know who the latest patrons of the local Turkish bathhouse are I'm sure she'll come to you," Kitty said with a glare.

It seemed there was bad blood between these two gossip mongers.

No surprises there.

Poor Jane was in her chair, thoroughly confused by Kitty's reference. Her pencil was still in the air, as though unsure if this was something she should be writing down.

Penelope coughed loudly to get their attention.

"I have four cats at home, three of whom provide enough fighting among themselves to satisfy my needs. If you two could retract your claws for a moment, we could return to the case that could very well keep me from going to prison for a crime I didn't commit?"

Benny's eyes grew in an exaggerated fashion and he pressed a hand to his chest. "Oh Pen, you poor dear. First, to have to be in the same room as that dreadful Constance, then, to be accused of her murder!"

"Speaking of people who might want her dead, I believe our Constance also had a bit of gossip with regard to you, didn't she Benny?" Kitty said, blinking her lashes at him.

He turned to give her a sardonic smile. "Constance knew better than to shoot across my bow."

"A naval reference? How appropriate."

"Children, *behave*," Penelope scolded, before focusing on Kitty again. "You were speaking about this Park Avenue First company?"

Benny pulled a chair closer and settled in, legs crossed and lips pursed. He eyed Kitty with all the approval of an angry wasp, but at least he remained quiet.

"Right," Kitty said importantly, shaking her head as though ridding herself of said wasp. "This Fredrick Carpenter has his eyes set on Park Avenue, but as you might imagine most of the property has long been held by old money, even as they decide to transform it into apartment buildings. Well, he has this grand idea of turning 4th Avenue into Park Avenue South."

"But what does that have to do with the Duke House?"

Kitty grinned. "That's the best part. Frederick bought the land between 32nd and 34th Streets, which is just south of where Park Avenue currently ends and turns into 4th

Avenue. Now see, he bought that property *knowing* that the current mayor would extend the original Park Avenue down to 32nd Street. Good old Freddie even went ahead and named his company Park Avenue First assuming he would have the address of 1 Park Avenue...which is currently held by—"

"The Duke House," Penelope finished in a gasp.

"Exactly. Now, here's where it gets interesting. The aldermen have moved the address back up, so the Duke House gets 1 Park Avenue again. It's been this whole back and forth between the mayor and the aldermen. Why is holding onto this address important to the Dukes? Because this Frederick fella has officially put his foot down and claimed that he wouldn't build anything along 4th Avenue unless, one, he gets the address of 1 Park Avenue and, two, he gets to name everything south of that Park Avenue South. If both those concessions are met, he plans on throwing everything he can at getting rid of the trolley car that currently runs down 4th Avenue to make it a more desirable street to live on."

"And the Dukes own the Empire Trolley Car Company, which I assume owns that line."

"Yep, and getting rid of the Park Avenue line would be disastrous for them. It would have a ripple effect on other lines throughout the city."

"Well, at least we know why the Dukes made an appearance at the luncheon. If they can preserve Duke House, including that address then there go Frederick Carpenter's plans."

"On the other hand, anyone who had a stake in the Park Avenue First corporation might have a motive for murder," Kitty said with satisfaction. "Which completely absolves the Dukes."

"Not necessarily," Benny interjected in a cool voice.

Everyone in the room turned to him.

"Stop with your banana oil," Kitty protested. "The Dukes had no reason to kill her. You just like creating controversy. Pen, we should go back and look at everyone at the table and instead of focusing on these silly bits of gossip Constance had on them, see if they or any of their family had a stake in Park Avenue First."

"It doesn't surprise me that you of all people would suggest that."

Kitty snapped her eyes back to him, narrowed with animosity. "And just what does that mean?"

"You know full well what it means," he said, suddenly serious. He turned to Pen as he extended one pointed finger Kitty's way. "This woman is not to be trusted Pen."

"Don't listen to him, he's just upset that you didn't include him in this. We all know how much he loves gossip."

"That I do," he said, reaching into the inside jacket of his pocket. "You don't mind if I have a cigarette, do you Pen?"

"I'd rather you—"

Pen stopped short when she saw the cigarette case he pulled out. It was inlaid with a geometric mother-of-pearl pattern—identical to the one Constance had in the courtyard.

"Where did you get that?"

Benny had been focused on Kitty, whose cheeks colored. He turned to Penelope with a bemused look. "*You* recognize it? Well, that's even better."

"Where did you get it?" she asked again, more insistently.

"This one? I bought it from Eleanor Winthorpe. She

seemed to have no desire to hold onto it. I only brought it along because Eleanor and Constance weren't the only two, *ahem*, paramours of John Duke who were blessed with such a gift from him." He turned to Kitty with a smirk. "Speaking of which, Kitty do you have a cigarette I can borrow? I seem to be plumb out."

Kitty was silent, seething in her seat.

"*You and John?*" Pen accused, turning to Kitty, eyes wide with surprise. She coughed out an incredulous laugh. "It all makes sense now."

"What does?" Kitty asked, looking defensive.

"All these secrets you *supposedly* held. They weren't exactly the most well-kept, were they? When we were at the table Marie already seemed to know about Alice. You teased her with a pun about construction work and Marie knew exactly what you were talking about. Heck, according to David, half of society probably knows about it. And this wager Marie had with Constance? Trust me, I know what goes into planning a wedding. My father oh so kindly reminded me when I called my own off. If Marie had a wedding planned for this spring and suddenly canceled, how many hundreds of people would know about it? It wouldn't take much for them to register that Constance was now having a spring wedding and Marie wasn't. And it wouldn't be too much of a stretch to tie it to their competition for the chair of the Young Ladies Historical Preservation Society. As for Eleanor, her history with John Duke is quite public, hardly even gossip fodder."

"What are you saying?"

"I'm saying that you've been plying me with information that, in retrospect, it wouldn't have taken me too long to discover on my own. All while cozying up to me and making sure I kept you in the loop about what I'd learned."

Now she was glad she hadn't yet told her about Alice or Eleanor. "And now it seems I know your real secret, Kitty. Is it true, you and John Duke have a secret affair going on?"

Her silence was enough of an answer.

"I rest my case," Benny said.

"Alright, yes, it's true," Kitty spat. "I'm admitting it, are you happy? It doesn't mean that I've been sabotaging this case, Pen. I wanted a story, that's all. I wasn't trying to undermine you."

"But you weren't honest with me either. I'll bet you were the one to tell Detective Beaks that I was gone those few minutes, also that I'd worked on a prior case involving poison, all the better to take the focus off you."

"What are you talking about? I never told him that. I didn't tell him anything about you."

"Why should I believe you? After keeping this from me? Something that you knew would make you even more of a suspect?"

"Why would I have told you? It's not even really a motive for murder. John and I both know it's not serious. I hadn't planned on *stealing* him from Constance. It's just a bit of fun. He's not even all that serious about her, he's just marrying her because his family likes the match."

"You're not exactly an unbiased source on that matter," Pen said.

Kitty shot up from her chair and glared at all of them, even poor innocent Jane, who was mesmerized with shock at everything that had been revealed. "Fine, go ahead and investigate me. I have nothing more to hide. I didn't kill Constance, and I'm certain you didn't either, Pen. I really was trying to help."

"And collect juicy tidbits for your silly little column," Benny interjected.

"Oh zip it, Benny," she seethed. She turned her attention to Penelope. "I suppose we're done here. Good luck with your investigation."

She stormed out, and Penelope felt a trickle of regret to see her go. She had actually been helpful in all of this. Still, now she looked more guilty than anyone else, and Penelope certainly had to factor that in.

"She was never going to tell you herself. You had a right to know something that might make her biased," Benny said, expressing Pen's own thoughts.

"You're right," she said with a sigh.

Jane looked perfectly flummoxed. "I always thought the rich were so sophisticated and proper, but they are awfully…"

"Shameless, dove, I know," Benny finished. He turned to Penelope. "So, what are you going to do now. Please tell me you'll start over with a focus on Kitty."

"What is it between you two?"

He pursed his lips and put Eleanor's cigarette case back into his jacket before answering. "Some sordid little story about the Turkish baths that landed a dear friend of mine who owns one into a bit of trouble."

"Gossip isn't so fun when it works against you."

"I only use mine for good," he said, fingertips pressed to his chest with indignation.

"Where should we go from here Miss Banks? Do you want to look into Miss Andrews?" Jane said.

"No, I want to talk with the Dukes first. John not only has some explaining to do but he might give me a name as to who would have a major stake in this whole Park Avenue business."

"In which case, I know exactly where to find him," Benny said with a smile. "Lucky for you, I'm here."

"Yes, it's certainly made my life less hectic," she said in a sardonic tone.

He tittered with amusement. "You'll be thanking me in a moment."

"Why is that?" she asked with suspicion.

"You'll see," he said with an enigmatic smile.

CHAPTER TWENTY-ONE

PEN AND BENNY WERE IN THE CAR AS LEONARD DROVE them to a still unknown address. Benny wouldn't tell Pen exactly where they were going and why she would be thankful he was with her. He'd always had a flair for the dramatic.

"So when did you buy Eleanor's cigarette case?"

"As soon as I heard a rumor that John and Kitty were involved," he said with a half-cocked smile. "I knew it would come in handy someday."

"You really have it in for her, don't you?"

"She's absolutely not to be trusted, Pen," he insisted. "Honestly, *that* is where I would have put all *my* efforts from the very start."

"She has been useful, Benny."

"And I'm sure filled her little notebook with scribbles she can use for the *New York Tattle*. I don't know why she wasn't fired after that fiasco about the bribing of public officials."

"How did you hear about *that*? It wasn't even published."

"I'm part of the idle rich, Pen. Gossip is how I fill my days. What else am I going to do, *work*?" He shuddered with revulsion at the idea of it.

Pen laughed softly and shook her head in wonder. Though, now that she thought about it, her job wasn't so different, especially with this case. Jane had a point, the wealthy may be sophisticated and proper by all outward appearances. Secretly, they made even the gangsters and card hustlers Pen once upon a time associated with seem like angels.

They ended up in front of a stately dark gray stone building that had the kind of facade, filled with scrolls and cornices, that would have the Young Ladies Historical Preservation Society salivating.

"The York Club?" Pen surmised, even though the only indication of what was housed inside was a small gold plaque near the door that she couldn't even read from the car. At least now it made sense why she would be glad Benny had come along.

The York Club was men only.

"How do you know John is here?"

"I'm not the only male member of the idle rich, Pen. At least a third of my gossip comes from this bountiful tap. John does enjoy a good high-stakes game of baccarat."

"Shouldn't he be in mourning?"

"Not if yesterday was any indication."

"*What*? He came here the day after Constance was murdered?" Pen asked in shock.

Benny simply raised one eyebrow as though that answered a hundred different questions.

"I suppose you had a point about focusing on the Dukes. Anyone who could be that callous surely deserves a closer look."

It also gave credence to what Kitty had said, that he didn't much care about the marriage to Constance. On the other hand, maybe he had been looking for a way out? Perhaps even to the point of murder?

"I'll go in and procure our suspect for you to interrogate."

"What makes you think you can lure him out?"

Benny pursed his lips. "I have my ways."

"Legal, I hope?"

"Pen, I'm offended. What do you take me for?"

"Should I answer that?"

He laughed and exited through the door Leonard held open for him. Penelope got out of the car and waited for him to return, hopefully with John in tow.

"You think this one will pan out, Miss Banks?"

She turned and saw just how concerned Leonard was. "Don't worry. I know I'm innocent, and the truth will at some point reveal itself."

At least she hoped so.

A few minutes later, Benny led John as they both exited through the front of the club, the latter sporting a resentful look on his face. His gaze narrowed with contempt when he saw Penelope waiting by the car. She didn't know what Benny had used as bait, but it must have had a bitter taste.

"I think we need to have a chat, John."

"I'll give you ten minutes, no more. Frankly, I shouldn't be talking to you at all. My lawyer would have a fit."

"My only aim is to clear a few things up. Better me than Kitty Andrews, no?"

She studied him for a reaction, which came in the form of a small twitch of the lips.

"The car should give us enough privacy."

Leonard instantly opened the car door for her.

"Only you, not Benjamin," he insisted, casting a sour look his way.

Benny gave an exaggerated pout but backed away.

Pen entered the car first and slid over so John could sit next to her. Leonard closed the door then joined Benny a few feet away to give them the requested privacy.

"I didn't kill Constance if that's what you're going to insinuate," he said before she could even ask a question.

"But you were cheating on her with Kitty."

He paused, studying her as though wondering how much to say. "It was nothing. Kitty understood that."

"Still, you gave her a cigarette case. The same as Constance? The same as Eleanor?"

He coughed out a sharp laugh. "Only because she insisted. I think for her it made the whole thing seem less—"

"Cheap and tawdry?"

He glared. "If that's how you want to put it. It didn't mean anything on my part. It was easy enough to buy her one. If it kept her complacent and quiet about our trysts, all the better."

"Did Constance insist on one as well?" Pen knew she liked to have what others had.

"Yes. She knew about the one I'd given to Eleanor and wanted the same. I made up some hokum about it being a token of my promise. It was enough to assure her parents that I would go through with the marriage. But with Eleanor, it was..." he glanced away.

"Love," Pen finished. This time she didn't need to say it in the form of a question. It was obvious from the look on his face.

"I know what everyone thought about the match, that she was too good for me, despite her family. She was so—I don't even know, beautiful and smart...untouchable. She was always lost in those books of hers. I think she preferred those silly little adventures to living them out in reality."

As a fellow book lover, Pen thought Eleanor had a point about being grateful Constance took John off her hands.

"She certainly never came sailing or racing with me. Even golf, which is my favorite. I would have thought she'd join me, if only to have some time outside to ourselves with something that wasn't too adventurous."

That explained Kitty's reference at the luncheon that seemed to rile Constance up so.

"Still, we got on well."

"But then she caught you and Constance together."

He blinked in surprise, then his face hardened in anger.

"She told me as much. On her *birthday*, John?"

"It was all Constance. She cornered me and, before I knew it, her lips were on mine!"

Penelope refrained from rolling her eyes. A likely story.

"I tried explaining that to Eleanor. At the very least I thought she would have forgiven me and gotten married if only to get at her trust, which was a lot more than the tiny bit she got at twenty-one. Otherwise, she doesn't get it until she's thirty."

Perhaps she valued her independence more, Penelope thought, admiring the young woman.

"That's why you were so uncomfortable at the luncheon. Eleanor, Kitty, and Constance in the same room?"

"That had nothing to do with it. I knew they'd be there. I told Kitty in passing. I even called Eleanor the week before in the hopes that..." He looked off to the side with a frown of disappointment.

Zounds, the boy was completely dizzy for the girl.

No doubt realizing Pen was observing him, he recovered, sitting up straighter to continue.

"It wasn't as though it was a secret that we were going to be there; the more people who knew ahead of time, the better. It was just such a tawdry dog-and-pony show we had to put on. The Dukes shouldn't have to stoop to that level just to protect their interests. It was undignified."

"Did you know Constance was…consorting with the gardener? Salvatore Rizzo."

His mouth curled up on one side and he breathed out a laugh. "I figure she was doing a lot more than that with him. Why do you think I never broke it off with Kitty? At least she isn't a flat tire, if you know what I mean."

Penelope could certainly surmise.

"Why were your parents so insistent on you marrying Constance?"

"They never liked Eleanor for me. Even though the Winthorpes wield a lot of power, it isn't the *noble* kind." He grimaced with annoyance. "But when it was insinuated that Constance had stolen me from her, both sides slammed the gavel on us."

"So you were reluctant to marry her?"

His gaze sharpened. "Not enough to kill her. Why would I? It was the epitome of convenience, we had an understanding. So yes, I knew about the gardener, even though she swore to be discreet." He twisted his lips in irritation, then continued. "And I had my own bit of fun."

This was pointless and her ten minutes were running out.

"The Duke House, it's currently sitting at 1 Park Avenue?"

A guarded look came to his face and he didn't answer.

"And the Dukes own a majority share of Empire Trolley Car Company?"

Now, he was completely closed off.

"I have reliable information that the Dukes have been bribing several aldermen and mayoral candidates all to prevent extending Park Avenue and renaming parts of 4th Avenue as Park Avenue South. But more importantly, to avoid doing away with the trolley car that runs down parts of it. That would mean a significant financial loss for the Dukes, no?"

An absolute lie, but Penelope was hoping to at least get a reaction.

His face was red with rage.

"That's slander! We haven't given one illegal cent to any mayoral candidate. Who are your sources? Was it that little—" His mouth immediately snapped shut. His eyes cooled into icy slits and his composure returned. "We Dukes have faith that whoever is elected for mayor will realize what makes this city run, and keep the trolley cars going, a convenience to the average New Yorker. Furthermore, any aldermen who *claim* to have been bribed are obviously working to sully our good name. We've always had the votes on our side, and after this upcoming election that won't change one bit."

"This Mickey Driver seems fairly popular. Based on his stance against trolly cars, I suspect Fredrick Carpenter who owns Park Avenue First has been throwing quite a bit of money at his campaign. Thus, if he wins, I doubt he'll vote to keep the Duke House at the 1 Park Avenue address."

"Driver," John sneered. "He won't win. The kinds of people he appeals to don't even know how to vote."

Pen was getting rather exhausted with the prejudice this case was revealing. Had she ever been this snobby?

Maybe those three years in jazz clubs and working a low-wage job had enlightened her.

Snobbery aside, she had noted that John had been rather adamant about not bribing any of the mayoral candidates. But he'd been more circumspect about the aldermen. It gave credence to the idea that illegal money was floating around in that segment of the political world.

"Don't think I don't know why you're really here, Penelope. You want to know if I killed Constance, and I've effectively destroyed any of your motives. I didn't care that she was cheating. And no, I wasn't enthusiastic about the marriage, but not enough to kill her, being that we had a perfect arrangement.

"Frankly, Constance being murdered has been disastrous for my family. The Gilmores include three aldermen. Do you have any idea how much influence that would have been? Furthermore, now the Young Ladies Historical Preservation Society probably won't take up our cause, not with Marie Phillips taking over as president. Her family has all but torn up the trolley car tracks already, just itching to use all that steel to build these ridiculous apartments everywhere. They have every reason to keep the Duke House from being preserved."

Except now that Marie was married, she would no longer be a member of the Young Ladies Historical Preservation Society. But John didn't know that—did he?

"The day Constance and I got engaged our company's share price went through the roof. It went up even more when the wedding was moved to an earlier date, mostly to get ahead of this election. So unless I am, for some absurd reason, shorting the stock in my own family's company, you have zero motive, Penelope."

He opened the car door and left before she could even respond.

Penelope was too absorbed in something he'd said; shorting his own family's company stock.

Her father was in finance, specifically investment and securities. As such, she had picked up certain things growing up, especially with her unique ability to remember what she read and saw. She knew enough on the topic to know what shorting a stock meant. It was when one "borrowed" stock in a company at a higher price and immediately "sold" it. The hope was that the price would go down in the near future, so one could "buy" back the shares at the lowered price, return them to the original owners, and personally recoup the difference. It worked to the borrower's advantage because they didn't have to put up any money to initially buy the stock, they could just "borrow" the shares. However, if the stock didn't go down quickly enough as planned they could lose money, potentially a ruinous amount.

If the price went up from the wedding announcement and went up even more from the new wedding date, anyone who knew it might suddenly and drastically drop in price— say from the very lucrative wedding being unequivocally terminated—would have made a killing.

Perhaps they had literally killed to accomplish it?

If Constance had actually saved the Duke House, all bets would be off. It would be permanently housed at 1 Park Avenue. Thus, Frederick would give up all his plans for 4th Avenue, including getting rid of the trolley car line.

So who had the most to gain? Perhaps someone whose father was in the automobile industry and would love to see an end to trolley cars. Someone who had been sent to the luncheon at the behest of their father. Someone who may have felt bitter about being the other woman.

"Please tell me he confessed everything," Benny said in a dramatic way when he stepped into the car to take the seat John had just vacated.

Penelope turned to him, now that the pieces were falling into place. "No, I think you were right, it may have been Kitty."

Benny blinked, his face blank for a moment. Then he breathed out a laugh. "*Zut alors*, Pen, I was mostly teasing when I suggested it was her, vicious little kitty-cat that she is, but now I'm curious."

Leonard was back in the car and Pen told him to drive back to her office. Then she turned to Benny to answer his question.

"This wedding, like many among our set, is as much business as it is love. In this case, more one than the other it seems. John mentioned that the only ones who'd make money from it not happening are people who had shorted stock in the Empire Trolley Car Company. Which gave Kitty not only motive but means and opportunity."

"How so?"

"Okay, let's start from where it likely began, the affair. I think she started this affair with John in the hopes that it would make Constance jealous enough to cancel the wedding. She even pressed him for her own cigarette case as evidence of the affair. Kitty didn't realize that John and Constance had an understanding with each other. Constance wouldn't have cared about him cheating."

"You don't say!" Benny said with delight.

Pen ignored him and continued. "Then, I think she tried to sabotage the company with a story about political bribes. That didn't work either since the story was killed ahead of time. Then when she learned John would be at the luncheon, she knew that if the Young Ladies Historical Preservation Society saved the house it would make it nigh impossible for Park Avenue First to get the address it wanted, so she got desperate and resorted to drastic means. Switching the place cards at the table was a genius move. It provided several far more likely suspects to take the blame, including myself." Penelope felt her anger grow at that, wondering how she had ever trusted the woman.

"So *money* was the motive all along?"

"Exactly," Pen said with grim satisfaction.

His heavy sigh he exhaled drew her attention.

"What is it?"

"You're ignoring one thing. As much as I would love to see the wretched kitten hang—well, not really, but maybe squirm a bit—money as a motive doesn't work. She turns twenty-five this year, same as you. Except, she hasn't upset daddums the way you have," he said with a wry grin. "That's five-hundred thousand on her birthday, and a hundred thousand clams every year after that. That's enough kale to sate even a voracious appetite like my own."

Penelope felt the wind go out of her sails. She fell back in disappointment, knowing that it must be true if Benny was the one telling her. When it came to the upper crust, scandal, and money, he might as well be the *New York Tattle* himself. Five hundred thousand was most definitely a lot of kale, certainly more than Kitty could have recouped playing a risky game like shorting a stock, not to mention the riskier move of murder.

"Then who the devil could it be?" Pen exclaimed, feeling her exasperation set in. At this point, she felt like arresting herself simply because even she felt she was the most likely suspect.

"Don't give up, dove," Benny said, patting her hand. "We'll work this out. Somewhere out there is the truth, and if anyone can find it, it's you."

Pen wasn't feeling all that optimistic. Yes, she'd had setbacks before, but never before had her neck been so close to the chopping block.

When Leonard parked the car in front of the building where her office was and opened the door for her the look of utter despondency must have shown. He gave her a sympathetic, yet encouraging smile. She couldn't muster up enough gumption to offer one back.

Pen allowed Benny to practically drag her back to the office.

They were met by an overly agitated Jane who accosted them as soon as they stepped foot in the door.

"Oh, thank god you're back. Detective Prescott called. They've arrested someone for the murder!"

CHAPTER TWENTY-TWO

"They're arresting the wrong person!"

Detective Prescott's eyes rolled up from his desk on the second floor of the 10A precinct police department. As usual, even Penelope's animated approach and announcement did nothing to disturb his patented equanimity, tinged by the barest amount of amusement.

"Miss Banks, disturbing the tranquility of the 10A as usual. I can only imagine what subterfuge you used to get past the officer on the first floor this time."

"This is no time to be glib," she said, boldly taking the seat near his desk. "What evidence do they have to make an arrest?"

Detective Prescott sat back in his seat to study her. "You realize this isn't my case, don't you? This isn't even a case for my precinct."

"Yet, you called to inform me all the same," she said. She momentarily reflected on what that meant, and couldn't deny the degree of pleasure that gave her, despite the circumstances.

"I assumed you'd want to know, being that you were a

suspect yourself. I would think you'd be glad the suspicion had been taken off you."

"I am, but not at the expense of an innocent party."

He studied her for a moment, his jaw hardening. "How are you so certain this suspect isn't the guilty party?"

She realized he was jealous and this time she couldn't hold back the enjoyment of it, again despite the circumstances.

"Salvatore Rizzo is an easy scapegoat. Surely you must know that. The detectives had it in for him from the very beginning. Those two mugs probably didn't even bother looking into any other suspect, not with the daughters of New York's wealthiest at stake."

"You won't find me disparaging any of my fellow detectives, but...that isn't beyond the realm of plausibility. However, even they wouldn't make an arrest without enough to make it stick."

"Which was?"

"Since I preemptively suspected you might charge in like a bee-stung bull—"

"You do know how to flatter a woman, Detective Prescott."

"—I took the liberty of learning the details. The analysis of the poison has come back. No one outside the department knows this, so keep it to yourself but it was sulfuric acid. It's used for various purposes in gardening, herbicide, pesticide, fertilizer. He had plenty of it available to him, and there was a store of it in a supply closet at the Peyton Foundation House."

"So anyone could have accessed it?"

"If they even knew it was there. Also, news has come to light that he was in an illicit relationship with the deceased."

"Illicit?" Penelope breathed out a cynical laugh. "Is that how they put it? Because he was of Italian heritage?"

"I presume because Miss Gilmore was engaged to be married," he said dryly.

"So what are they claiming is the motive?"

"When it comes to relationships, the possibilities are almost endless."

"That's an awfully pessimistic view of relationships."

"Says the woman who scoffs at marriage."

"I suppose murder is one more reason to avoid it."

"Perhaps he grew weary of her barging into his workplace," Detective Prescott arched an eyebrow and gave Pen a pointed look.

"I would hope if a man grew that weary of *me*, he'd resort to something other than poison," Penelope said, arching an eyebrow of her own.

"I suppose some men have a much higher tolerance level."

Pen twisted her lips in reluctant amusement.

Then she remembered why she was there.

"I have a new and even more likely motive for murder."

"I have to say, at least when you barge in, you come bearing gifts. What is this motive?"

"Money, naturally. Constance's murder, or rather her marriage, is tied to the election and the trolley cars and Park Avenue and...well, it's somewhat complicated."

"It sounds complicated."

"But it certainly makes more sense than a gardener killing her, and for what reason? A fit of passion? Her trying to end it? Jealousy? I doubt this young man has ever suffered from any of those maladies."

Penelope was glad to see Detective Prescott's eyes narrow in a way that hinted at his own jealousy.

"I don't think he did it, Richard."

His eyes flashed with irritation at the use of his first name, darting from side to side as though worried someone had heard her.

"Oh stop, no one is paying attention to me."

"I doubt that very much," he said, his eyes settled back on her.

Pen idly brushed back a strand of hair, which she always did when he managed to obliterate her composure.

"Okay, *Detective Prescott*. At any rate, I always took you for a man who believed in justice. You didn't even cross me off the list in a prior case when it was perfectly obvious to everyone else I hadn't done it."

"Everyone else wasn't as objective as I was."

"And where is that man now?"

"That man is wondering why you think this Salvatore Rizzo is so innocent."

"I just...do. I know that doesn't fit with your idea of being a proper detective."

"Actually, I'm a firm believer in hunches."

The word wasn't familiar to Pen but she understood the context. "If I could talk to him maybe I could help clear it up."

"What makes you think he'll talk to you?"

"Innocent men should be eager to defend themselves no? It can't hurt to ask."

He studied her for a beat. "I'm going to regret this, aren't I?"

"You always say that and it always works out."

He sighed then nodded. "Okay, let's plead our case."

Detectives Beaks and Reynolds were understandably reluctant at first, especially when they learned it would be a woman speaking to their jailed suspect.

Detective Prescott showed far more charm and congeniality than Penelope would have in getting them to agree. She had learned from her very first murder case that men had an unfortunate habit of considering their fellow man more favorably than they did the fairer sex. Thus, she knew when to shut up and let the men do the talking, as much as it rankled her.

Still, ten minutes later she and Detective Prescott were in their own interrogation room with one Salvatore Rizzo. Pen would have preferred he not be there, but he made it quite clear that he would never *ever* leave her alone in a room with a murder suspect. As patronizing as it was, she didn't entirely hate that of him.

Poor Salvatore wasn't looking quite so handsome today. He was paler and looked as though he'd lost ten pounds overnight. His eyes were wide and almost feral and the growth of beard darkening his cheeks didn't help make him look any less like a sinister character.

"I should make it clear that nothing you tell us is confidential and may be used against you in a court of law," Detective Prescott initiated.

Salvatore nodded absently, staring at the hands that were twisted together on the table, still in handcuffs.

Detective Prescott shifted his gaze to Penelope.

"Salvatore," she said gently. She had to repeat his name just to get him to look at her. "I don't think you did this, but it would help if you could tell me anything that could help your case?"

"I *didn't* do this! I told you, me and Constance? It was just a bit of fun. Nothing serious. I knew that! I wasn't expecting anything more from it. The things they're accusing me of? It's disgusting. Why would I do that?"

He was getting overly agitated. Next to her, she could feel Detective Prescott go tense.

"Okay, okay," she said gently, trying to calm him down.

He went silent but his breathing came in heavy.

"Did she give you any hint that someone may have wanted her dead? Maybe that someone didn't want the wedding to happen?"

He shook his head again. "Like I told you, we didn't talk weddings." His eyes flashed and then quickly diverted away, as though there was more he had to say.

"What is it?"

His gaze solidified as he brought it back to her. "Nothin'."

"Salvatore," she said in a stern voice, the kind teachers used when students were fibbing. "You are about to be tried for murder. *Murder*. Now is not the time to keep something to yourself that might absolve you."

He held her gaze for a moment, then lowered his eyes to stare at the table.

"What is it?"

"I don't want to get her into trouble. She didn't do this either."

Both Pen and Detective Prescott sat up straighter at that.

"Who?"

"Well, me and Constance, it was fun, yeah? But, it wasn't just...you know. We had another arrangement."

"Which was...?"

He hesitated again.

Zounds, this was as tedious as waiting for Christmas to arrive!

"All that stuff she knew about them other girls, I was the one to tell her."

"What?" This was certainly a surprise. "How the devil did you have so much information?"

He twisted his mouth to the side. This was obviously the thing he wanted to keep private.

Penelope went through all the women involved and landed on the most obvious one.

"Was it Kitty? Katherine Andrews who told you?"

"The one with the red hair? Nah, not her."

Yet another mark in favor of Kitty's innocence. She moved on and landed on...

"Eleanor! Surely it was her, her family owns most of the newspapers in the city if not the country."

Nothing in Salvatore's expression indicated she was the right one. He still looked hesitant.

Good grief, she'd have to go through the whole attendee list before—

"*Mabel?*" she asked, incredulous.

His eyes flashed wide, telling her that was the right answer.

She recalled his using her first name back in the library before correcting himself. Pen now briefly wondered if there was something even more there. But that salacious bit could wait.

"How did she know so much?"

He shrugged.

"All's I knows is she'd give me the information. Some of it was...." He shook his head in wonder and breathed out a short, humorless laugh. "Anyways, that was that. I know how Constance used it, and I feel kinda bad about that."

Penelope was still reeling with this news, trying to figure out how Mabel knew so much. She knew women like her could be treated as nothing more than background furniture, as was often the case with staff. People spoke freely in front of them as though they weren't even there. Still, even the most reckless member of high society would have to be daft to let some of the things Pen had learned while working on this case slip out of their mouths.

"That doesn't mean I killed her! Why would I? Neither did Mabel," he insisted, a hard edge to his voice.

"How did this even start?"

He gave Penelope a sheepish look. "In my job, I hear stuff. You'd be surprised the things people say when you're nothing more than some 'dago' gardener trimmin' the rose bushes," he glowered with resentment at the slur. "Most of it's nonsense, but Constance always got a laugh out of hearing it. Sometimes, she'd even pay me. With this Young Ladies Society whatever, I knew she was using it against some of them, so I stopped. Mostly because Mabel told me it was wrong."

Again, he paused, his brow wrinkling in confusion.

"Which is why it was so strange when Mabel suggested I start telling Constance things again. Only now Mabel was the one giving me the information. I have no idea why, or how. But that don't mean she's not a good woman. I know she didn't kill Constance. She's been real good to me, you know?" A crooked grin came to his face which told Penelope there were several different meanings for the word "good."

Detective Prescott deliberately cleared his throat.

"Sorry," Salvatore said, looking so much like a five-year-old that Penelope felt herself soften. It occurred to her that this kind of charm was part of what made him so attractive.

Right now her mind was on Mabel, who obviously had an agenda.

But she wanted to be thorough, not dismissing Salvatore until she was certain.

"Where did you and Constance disappear to after meeting in the courtyard?"

His eyes warily flashed to Detective Prescott then back to Pen. He shrugged and grinned. "Where do you think? To get some privacy."

"And this sulf—sulfuric—"

"Sulfuric acid," he finished for her. "It was kept in an unlocked closet; *anyone* coulda gotten to it."

"Did Mabel have any gossip to give you that day?"

He shook his head. "Nah, it only happened a few times last year."

"When?"

He thought about it. "Before the meeting during the summer was the first time. From then, it kept coming in, and the last time was before the next meeting in the fall. Constance was real jazzed about that election, she knew she was gonna win."

So did Mabel Colton.

"So...am I off the hook now?" he asked hopefully.

She didn't want to get his hopes up, but she also didn't want to destroy his last bit of optimism. "I'm going to find out."

She rose, and Detective Prescott did the same. They left the room.

Detective Beaks and Detective Reynolds were there, looking more satisfied than ever.

"None of that does anything to clear his name, you realize. I still think we have our guy," Detective Beaks said, sneering at Penelope.

"We'll see," she said, hoping her smile didn't look too

impudent. Mostly she wanted to leave before she did or said something she'd regret.

Once outside again, she exhaled, happy to be away from them.

"Let me guess, the next step is to question this Mabel Colton?" Detective Prescott said.

"Naturally," Penelope said.

CHAPTER TWENTY-THREE

"The truth is, I have no idea from whom the information came."

Mabel was understandably defensive when Detective Prescott and Pen confronted her. Only when they mentioned Salvatore did she relent, turning red in the process.

"How did you get the information?" Detective Prescott asked.

"Letters addressed to me here."

"And you decided to forward the information to Salvatore?"

"The letters instructed me to do that."

"And you just did it without question?" Pen asked, incredulous.

Mabel lifted her chin a bit higher. "I didn't see the harm in it. I was told to pass the information on to him. I had no idea he'd be telling Constance, or how she'd use the information."

"You're being disingenuous," Pen scolded.

Mabel at least had the tact to look slightly abashed. Her

hand rose to fiddle with diamond folds in the bib of her black and gold dress. Art Deco was seeping its way into fashion. Penelope recognized it from a recent trip to Lord & Taylors, which wasn't exactly the most affordable place for someone like Mabel to—

"How much money were you making from this?" Penelope asked.

Mabel's eyes widened only briefly before returning to normal, but Pen caught it. "What are you talking about?" She said with a small laugh. "How would I possibly make money from this?"

"The marriage. You knew that if Constance Gilmore and John Duke married it would secure trolley cars and rail lines throughout the city, maybe even expand them. The information you somehow got a hold of and forwarded only bolstered that idea, since Constance would become chairlady and thus protect the Duke House. You could easily make money in the stock market on any one of the Dukes' holdings."

Mabel laughed and shook her head. It looked genuine.

"Oh my dear, that truly is funny. What would a woman like me be doing in the stock market?" All hints of humor left her face as she gave Pen a steady gaze. "I don't come from family money like some. I make a pittance working here. The only benefit is that I get free boarding for playing housekeeper. I have to do most of the cleaning myself of course. If I had any extra money, I certainly wouldn't put it in the stock market."

"But you *were* getting paid," Detective Prescott said.

That had an altogether different effect.

Mabel considered him for a moment and Pen was prepared for another denial. Instead, she relaxed and exhaled. "Yes, I was getting paid. So what? Again, it isn't a crime."

"But murder is," Pen said.

Mabel offered a humorless smile. "Why on earth would I kill Constance? Yes, she was an odious little minx, but I had no reason to kill her. Whoever was paying me might have decided to resume paying me to provide her with information in the future, in which case I had every reason to keep her alive."

"So you *did* know it was being forwarded to Constance!" Pen accused.

Mabel's jaw hardened for a moment before she relented.

"Okay yes, I knew. That was part of the instruction in fact. But again, it only supports the idea that I didn't kill her. She had *some* use for me. She was saving the Duke House, which only bode well for this place. The Peyton Foundation Home is under the same scrutiny. Do you think I haven't heard talk about plans for 4th Avenue? Why do you think I was so willing to accept the money? I had to protect myself for the day when this place closes its doors."

"So you didn't have enough to invest in the stock market, but you had no qualms spending it on nice clothes, *expensive* clothes, despite being worried about your future?" Penelope said, eying her dress. "That either makes you incredibly irresponsible, or you knew there was more money coming in. Say from shorting the stock in the Empire Trolley Car Company?"

"Shorting the stock? What does that even mean?" Mabel said, throwing up her hands in exasperation.

"Feigning ignorance won't hold up in a court of law, Miss Colton," Detective Prescott warned her.

"Go through my finances! My bank account, anything!"

"Money can easily be hidden if you're smart enough."

Panic finally set in. "Oh no, I am not going to prison for this. No, no, no."

"Mabel, right now they've arrested Salvatore for this. Is it fair for him to go to prison for this when you know he did nothing?"

She looked ready to argue further, then something in her gaze changed. She sighed and brought one hand up to her forehead and closed her eyes as though a sudden headache had hit.

"I...may be able to absolve him."

"Then do it," Penelope pleaded. "What information do you have?"

Mabel opened her eyes and looked at them, reluctance in her gaze.

"Miss Colton, if you have evidence related to the crime, I have to insist that you provide it."

"It's a letter. The same as the others, which I also held onto." Her hand fell away and she averted her gaze. "I received another thousand dollars and the promise of a hundred dollars every month if I made sure the punch was already poured at the tables before the luncheon started."

"*What?*" Both Pen and Detective Prescott exclaimed at the same time.

"And you didn't think *that* was suspicious?"

"How could I have known it would lead to poison? There could have been any number of reasons for the request."

"Not really," Pen said, giving her a withering look.

"All the same, it isn't criminal."

"Keeping that information from the police could be," Detective Prescott said. "A charge of aiding and abetting might also potentially be applied."

"Why do you think I didn't tell anyone? I knew how it would look. The finger would surely be pointed at me. Salvatore knew about me providing the information, and those detectives would have been all too happy to browbeat it out of him."

"You'll be happy to know he kept the information to himself. He only told me because I pressed him. He's been protecting you, Mabel."

She swallowed. "Why do you think I'm giving you this now? I don't want him to go to prison for this. Despite his... tendency to play around and his questionable choices in partners, he's a sweet boy at heart."

"I'll need that letter, and the others that you have," Detective Prescott insisted.

She nodded and left to retrieve them.

"This could be it!" Penelope said, getting excited. "If we can determine who wrote the letter, we have our killer."

"I wouldn't get too excited. This person was smart enough to remain anonymous. I doubt they'd be stupid enough to send a letter that left a trace of who they are. I suspect the writing will be block lettering and there'll be no fingerprints."

"Always the pessimist," Penelope said. She paced around the foyer, releasing her pent up energy.

Her eyes caught a glimpse of the library. The light came through the stained glass René Gauthier doors that looked so similar to the ones in her apartment. They were closed against the sun that filtered through, and the color danced across the furniture and books. Penelope walked over to admire them. She wondered what would happen to them if this place was torn down. With a sigh, she turned and looked around the room at the furniture and books. It was crazy to think that only a few days ago—

Penelope's breath caught.

Her mind raced back in time, focusing on one particular moment in the library. Pen filtered it through everything else she'd learned, and everything each suspect had said.

"Zounds!" She almost slapped her forehead at how oblivious she'd been. "The pearls!"

Penelope rushed back to the foyer.

Mabel had come back with the letters, and they were all laid flat on a console table next to the envelopes they had been sent in.

Detective Prescott was staring down at the most recent that had requested the punch be served early. Pen briefly noted that the stamp for that one was different from the others, violet and square-shaped instead of red and rectangular.

"It's as I suspected, whoever sent these letters used block lettering," he said. "We'll never be able to compare it with a handwriting sample. There's also no return address on the envelopes."

Pen had figured as much, but it no longer mattered.

"Never mind that, I think I know who killed Constance. I just have to prove it."

"You do?" Mabel asked, eyes squinted with uncertainty.

Even Detective Prescott gave her a doubtful look.

"It all started with the pearls," Pen said excitedly.

"That clarifies nothing," he said.

Penelope grabbed his arm. "Let's go, I need to confirm something."

"Wait, the letters," he said, pulling out a handkerchief. He carefully put each letter back in its envelope. He wrapped them all in the handkerchief, then allowed Pen to drag him out of the building.

Once outside, she said, "I didn't want to reveal anything

in front of her. I'm still not sure but there's enough to make me damn suspicious."

"Care to give me a name? Or at least a hint?"

"To do that I need to explain everything from the beginning."

Leonard had driven them to the Peyton Foundation House and she led the detective back to the car.

"I'll tell you everything on the trip down to Wall Street." She stopped suddenly and sighed with resignation. "I need to talk to my father."

CHAPTER TWENTY-FOUR

By the time Leonard parked in front of the office building where Penelope's father worked on Wall Street, she had explained all the relevant points to Detective Prescott, including the name of who she thought had killed Constance.

"Are you sure about the details?"

She gave him a half-cocked smile. "By now you should know how well my memory works." She twisted her lips to the side. "I just need to be better at using it to put those clear images together to solve the puzzle more quickly."

"For someone who's been a detective for only a few months, I'd say you're doing dammed well."

She smiled, then exited the car when Leonard opened the door for them. The smile disappeared when she turned to look at the office building. The firm where her father was a partner was housed on the top several floors, and she hadn't been there in years. Even before their schism, she had rarely visited him at work.

Although she ultimately wanted to speak to her father alone, bringing Detective Prescott with her did serve a purpose. Now, she was glad to have him by her side simply for the emotional support it offered, not having to enter this lion's den alone.

They went through the front doors and took the elevator up to the floor where her father's office was. She was surprised to recognize the face of the woman at the receptionist desk in front.

"Miss Banks!" Martha Blackbird greeted, her face brightening with pleasure. "I haven't seen you here in years. Look at you, a proper young lady now."

She eyed the man next to her and a knowing smile came to her lips. "And you've brought a handsome young man with you. Here to see your father I presume?"

Penelope allowed the presumption to stand, realizing that explaining would just waste time. In her periphery, she noted the subtle smile of amusement on the lips of the "handsome young man."

"We are. I assume he's in his office?"

"Of course. Just let me call and see if he's available."

This was new. Usually, Penelope was able to walk right in. The surprise must have shown on her face.

"A new system. You've been gone too long, my dear," Martha said with a mockingly censuring look. "Ever since that mess with the bombing, there are all kinds of checks in place."

Penelope could only think of one "mess with the bombing" and that had been back in 1920 right here on Wall Street. Zounds, it really had been a long time since she'd been here.

"Hello, Sarah, you'll never guess who is here to see Mr. Banks. It's his daughter, and she's brought a young man with her," she added in a confidential tone.

"Detective Richard Prescott," Penelope whispered.

Martha's eyes widened with acknowledgment. "He's a detective, Mr. Richard Prescott."

Once again, Penelope allowed the misinterpretation to stand. Martha apparently thought Penelope had a more intimate relationship with the detective than was true. At the very least, it would make her father curious enough to at least grant them access.

Martha silently nodded and hung up.

For one horrid moment, Penelope thought her father would be brash enough to dismiss her without granting an audience.

"Go right on through, dear. You do remember the way don't you?" She teased.

"Of course, and it's so good to see you again Mrs. Blackburn."

"You should visit more often, especially once the little ones arrive."

"Pineapples," Penelope muttered under her breath as they left.

Detective Prescott laughed softly.

Sarah, another familiar face, was already standing to greet them by the time they made it past a sea of curious eyes and many a double-take.

"Miss Banks, it's so good to see you," she greeted in a more professional manner. Her eyes landed on the man next to her. "And you must be Detective Richard Prescott?"

"I am."

Her smile grew ever so slightly and she gestured to the open door beyond. "If you'll follow me."

"Actually," Penelope said, "I should talk to my father alone." She turned to Detective Prescott, apologetically. She did feel bad for using him to draw enough curiosity and interest to help ease her way to this point. "There are some family matters I need to discuss with him."

Detective Prescott, to his credit, simply nodded with understanding and took a step back.

If Sarah had any questions, she was tactful enough to keep the curiosity from her face. Once inside her father's office, she left and closed the door behind Penelope.

Pen took a moment to look around, noting that almost nothing had changed since she was last here. But that was her father to a fault, he had never liked change. He had a corner office, naturally, since he was a senior partner in the investment firm, and she could see the East River and Brooklyn beyond that on one side and a view of Wall Street from another.

"I suppose this time I'm the one wondering to what I owe the honor of a visit with my daughter," Her father greeted, looking far more suspicious than pleased to see her.

Pen turned her attention back to him and pursed her lips. "Oh papa, let's not pretend you don't know what's happened this past week. I'm sure your heartburn powder supply has suffered for it."

"That's been the case since you learned to walk and talk."

She sighed and took a seat across from him.

"This detective, is he here in some...custodial capacity?"

"No," Penelope said idly, enjoying how much the curiosity was grating on him.

"Then am I to make certain...*other* assumptions?"

"No," she said, inadvertently coughing out a laugh.

He exhaled with impatience. "If you came simply to be bothersome, Penelope, I'll have to ask you—"

"I have a request."

He paused. "Which is...?"

"With regard to Constance's murder, as you might imagine, I am a suspect, a *prime* suspect."

"My understanding is that they've arrested someone," he said, his brow wrinkled with confusion.

Penelope stared at him in surprise. The only way he'd know that is if he had taken the trouble to make inquiries. And the only way he'd have done that is if he had actually cared about the case at all, or at least his own daughter.

After their history, Penelope wasn't about to give him that much credit so easily. Most likely he was worried about his own image if his daughter had indeed committed the crime.

Something she could use to her advantage.

"Actually, new evidence has come to light and they'll be releasing that suspect soon. He's innocent. The detective outside can confirm for you," she lied.

His look of suspicious consternation didn't go away.

"Which is why I've come to you, papa," she said, her head and eyelids demurely lowering as she twiddled her fingers in her lap.

"Penelope, I've been immune to your pretenses since you were ten years old. The innocent act no longer works on me. Tell me what it is you've come to ask of me since we both know this isn't simply a dear daughter calling on her beloved father."

Penelope exhaled and lifted her head and eyes once again. She should have known better.

"We both know that all you care about is image, so I've come to do you the favor of helping protect that image."

He breathed out a laugh. "And we both know that you care not one iota about my image or your own for that matter, so what are you really after?"

Penelope thought about being perfectly direct but

figured with her father some foundation would need to be settled first.

"What do you know about the election?"

He raised an eyebrow in surprise. "I know quite a bit about the election. I'm surprised to learn that *you* even know there's an election this year. I suppose we have the suffragettes to blame for that."

"Dastardly women," Penelope said with mock scorn.

"Why do you want to know about the election?" he asked with irritation.

"You're an alderman, no?"

Again, he looked surprised, then suspicious. "Yes."

"The Duke House, has there been much debate about it?"

"So that explains it." He studied her for a moment. "To answer your question, yes, it has been hotly debated, and I know all the reasons why. I'm no advocate for change just for the sake of change, but the Dukes are fighting an uphill battle and unwinnable war. I couldn't care less whether Park Avenue starts at 32nd or 34th Street. I also couldn't care less about what 4th Avenue is called. However, I do understand investment growth. There's money to be made in building apartments, and absolutely none to be made holding onto empty mansions that serve little purpose."

"And the trolley car lines?"

"A dying nuisance, thankfully. Not that I'm all that enamored of cars, especially the way some people drive. However, the future is cars, aeroplanes as well, both of which are advancing faster than I would have thought. Two growing industries I've been keeping my eye on. I suspect one day, every American will have their own car, perhaps even their own aeroplane, though I'm not sure how that would be regulated. Still, people appreciate actual ownership of things."

"So I assume you voted to extend Park Avenue for Frederick Carpenter?"

"Naturally."

"Do you think other aldermen were bribed to vote differently?"

His gaze narrowed, the blue eyes she had inherited from him going hard.

"I have nothing to confirm such a thing if that's what you're asking."

"But you suspect?"

"I'll deny it if anyone else comes back asking but...yes, I have my suspicions."

"And the bank involved? Would it be New York First Bank?"

"Again, I don't have proof, but there are murmurs. Honestly, I never trusted the lot of them, the Todds; snobbery personified. I know you were once friends with David Todd, but now that you have money, Penelope, trust me when I say don't entrust them with your money. They've been extending credit to some questionable international endeavors. Yes, Bavaria is ripe for the picking after that disastrous war that accomplished absolutely nothing, but why put your money behind some fascist upstart that is a laughing stock to the average German and Austrian? National Socialist something or the other, Nazi, I think it is. The very name is a joke, and my understanding is they are nothing more than thugs. Perhaps the Todds have faith in them eventually coming to power. I do not."

"And here in New York?" Penelope prodded.

"They prefer old money...and lately political money."

Which confirmed what Alice had said, and at least completed that puzzle.

"Is that all?" he hinted.

"No, that's not really what I came to request."

He closed his eyes and took a breath, no doubt to regulate his growing irritation. "Then what the devil is it you want from me?"

"I need to know who shorted a certain stock this week."

His eyes flashed open. "I beg your pardon?"

"Are you able to find that out? Even if another investment firm handled it?"

"I could, but it would be a gross violation of trust. Our clients rely on our discretion and the protection of their privacy. What on Earth made you think I would agree to something like that?"

"Someone shorted stock in the Empire Trolley Car Company, most likely this week. Someone who knew Constance would not be alive to marry John Duke and thus provide his family with the additional support they need to maintain their holdings, at least in any profitable way."

Understanding hardened his gaze as it penetrated her. "And you have proof of this?"

"I have quite a bit of circumstantial evidence that makes me think this is the case. The one missing piece of the puzzle is who actually shorted the stock. That would cement it."

"You realize what you're asking me to do is highly unethical. It could very well expose me to civil liability, maybe even criminal."

"I do," Penelope said apologetically. "I also know that an innocent boy, or potentially your own daughter, could go to prison solely because someone else got greedy and committed murder because of it."

He studied her for a long time. She was certain he was going to say no.

"I'm not going to give you an answer just like that. This is a very serious request, Penelope. Not one I'm sure I should indulge."

"I suppose I should leave it to your conscience to decide."

He worked his jaw and narrowed his eyes. "Yes, I suppose so."

They stared at each other for a moment. Pen had no idea what he was thinking or which direction he would decide, but she had her own debate going on. When it was settled in her head, she spoke.

"Do you know a Sylvine Jade?"

The reaction was quick, almost too quick to see, but Penelope caught it.

"It doesn't sound familiar," he blustered. "Where did you hear it?"

Penelope stared, a weak smile coming to her mouth. "I heard it in reference to my mother."

Now, he was angry. "From whom?"

"A performer."

The alarm that hit his gaze sent a shock through her. It disappeared quickly enough but it left her wondering.

"What performer?"

"No one you would know. He said he knew Mama by that name once upon a time. Was this when she was an actress? Or was she a singer? A dancer? Magician? Lion Tamer? I never got a real answer from any of you, even Mama, even Agnes Sterling, they wouldn't tell me anything!"

"Because it's none of your concern."

"I can handle it Papa, whatever it is," she pleaded. "I'm

not a little girl and I'm certainly not naïve, not after the past three years."

His eyes flashed in horror, no doubt thinking the worst of her and what she may have done during those three years.

Penelope laughed. "It's not very fun being kept in the dark about your own family, is it?"

He exhaled in anger.

"Yes, your mother once went by the name Sylvine Jade. She was..." he paused and seemed confused for a moment before continuing. "An actress, I suppose."

Penelope was so stunned by his confession (finally!) it took her a moment to process it. In her resulting silence, he continued.

"You now know everything you need to know. Her family was one she desperately tried to escape, and I was able to help with that. They were paid and *threatened* never to come near any of us ever again. Don't go seeking them out Penelope, you won't find what you're looking for unless that is pain and disappointment." He leaned in and gave her a direct look. "And it won't bring her back."

"But—"

"No." He put his hand up to stop her. "That's all I'll say on the matter."

Penelope opened her mouth to speak again, but the look on his was already closed off to further conversation.

She rose up and quickly left, not bothering to plead her case about the far more important request she had given him. She'd gotten an answer for the thing that had been eating her up for some time now, and it gave her...nothing.

Outside her father's office, she rushed past Detective Prescott who followed her to the elevators. They arrived quickly and the two of them entered, him keeping a respectful distance and silence.

She hadn't told him what she was going to ask her father for, knowing that it might very well be illegal. She hadn't wanted to compromise either of the two men in her life. She hiccuped a laugh as they went down, realizing what she had just thought to herself. The two men in her life.

Detective Prescott, true to his sometimes infuriatingly placid nature remained silent. She would have liked to introduce him to her father, if only so he'd realize she was capable of at least knowing one decent, upstanding person.

"I'll see what I can dig up on my own back at the 10A," he said, channeling how disappointing the meeting had been for her.

She gave him a grateful smile. "I'll have Leonard drop you off first. I'll be back at my office if you learn anything."

It was a silent and somber ride to both locations, and by the time Penelope got back to her own office, she was feeling more despondent than ever. All she had were—what had Detective Prescott called it?—hunches. No actual proof.

"Miss Banks, I received a phone call from a Mr. Banks? Is he related to you?" Jane said as soon as she walked through the front door.

"You did?" Penelope asked, rather than answering the question.

She briefly wondered how he knew about this business of hers, but dismissed that thought.

"What did he say?"

"He told me to tell you that there was only one buyer for the past two weeks, at least to any great amount—he didn't say what they were a buyer of—but it was a corporation called Minerva who had done the buying."

"Minerva? Are you sure?"

Jane checked her notepad and nodded. "I'm sure."

This answered nothing. Penelope sighed in bewilderment, thinking about everything she knew of the Roman Goddess.

Another thought occurred to Penelope. Her father had done this for her, despite the risk, despite his irritation and disappointment with her. Perhaps they could mend this rift after all.

"Does that mean anything to you?" Jane asked, drawing Penelope's attention again.

It came to her slowly, and yet another piece of the puzzle fell into place.

Penelope smiled. "It does. I know how we can find out for sure—and potentially catch our killer."

CHAPTER TWENTY-FIVE

ONCE AGAIN, PENELOPE FOUND HERSELF IN THE offices of the New York Tattle. She had made it past the security guard and disappointed the young woman at the front desk by coming up unannounced yet again.

She had a feeling the element of surprise was needed even more today.

When Penelope exited on the third floor, she saw Kitty furiously typing away at the typewriter on her desk. Considering the look on her face, she was getting her resentment and frustration out in the article she fully planned on writing now that she and Pen no longer had an agreement. No doubt Penelope Banks would come out looking guiltier than ever in that story.

"I pity whoever your victim is in that piece," she said by way of announcing her presence.

Kitty's only reaction was to stop typing for one second, as though she'd lost her rhythm, then continue on, more furiously than ever.

"I've come to say, that I don't think you're the murderer."

Kitty just raised one eyebrow and continued to focus on her typing.

"I've also come to say that I know who it is, and I have proof."

This was enough to get her to stop fully. She continued to stare at the paper without further acknowledgment.

"If all you want is an apology, then I'll give it, but is that really fair?"

Kitty's eyes snapped up to hers. "Yes, as a matter of fact, it is."

"Why? You *did* keep something from me, something rather important."

"And you certainly kept plenty from me."

"Only out of necessity or circumstance."

"Ha!" she spat out and resumed typing.

"Okay, I suppose I'll take my information to the *New York Times* and—"

"Stop," Kitty said, the sound of her typing going quiet.

Pen folded her arms over her chest and waited.

"What do you have?"

"Actually, it's what *you* can have. That bit of subterfuge you pulled with Marie? I need you to do it again."

"Is she the one who—*wait!*"

Pen started in surprise at the outburst.

Kitty looked around suspiciously, then took Penelope's arm and walked her back to the room with the telephone. Once the door was closed she confronted her.

"Who is it you think did it?"

"First let me ask you something."

"Okay?" Kitty said, understandably guarded.

"This story of yours about the bribery when did you start working on it?"

"A few weeks ago."

"And what was the story?"

"I just knew that certain aldermen were getting bribes. I had an initial list of names and a source, who I still won't name out of integrity, but I can confirm he worked for one of the aldermen. He's the one who changed his mind just when I was getting started. Something scared him, even though I promised never to reveal him as a source."

"And you never knew why they were getting bribes and from whom?"

"No, before I could even get that far, my source reversed his story. My editor wouldn't let me go near it again so I dropped it."

"Were any of these aldermen getting bribed by one of the Gilmores?"

"No."

"That's understandable, the Dukes already had them in their pocket."

"The *Dukes*? What do they have to do with this?"

Penelope scrutinized her. "You didn't happen to tell John about this story prior to publication, did you?"

"It wasn't as though it was top secret—" The color drained from Kitty's face, then the blood came racing back with a vengeance. "*He* was the one to get the story canceled?"

"The Dukes were the entire reason these aldermen were getting bribed."

"Crackers! *That's* why Constance knew. I knew that lying bastard told her, despite his protests. The two of them probably threatened everyone who worked for any of the bribed aldermen hoping the right one would renege. Well, it worked."

"This should be a lesson in keeping your mouth shut, perhaps? Even for things that aren't 'top-secret.'"

"Did you come here to scold me?" Kitty snapped.

"No, I want to know how you got the information."

"It was from a letter sent to me."

Penelope grinned. "And I'm sure you held onto it?"

"Of course, I had to protect myself. It's the only reason I wasn't fired." Without Pen's prodding, Kitty rushed to go and get it.

When she brought the letter back, Penelope noted that the writing was the same block lettering on high-quality cream paper that Mabel had received. This envelope also had the same violet square stamp of the most incriminating of Mabel's letters.

Now Pen took a closer look at the stamp. She instantly recognized it as a special Victory Issue 3-cent stamp. Odd, since the cost of postage was only 2 cents, as were the red stamps on most of the letters Mabel had received. In fact, Pen hadn't seen one of these stamps in years. More to the point, why would someone use it for these letters in particular?

Pen had a moment of doubt, wondering if it had been two different people who had sent the letters. But everything else, even the block lettering was identical, so they had to be the same person. Right?

"Someone definitely wanted to use you to ruin the Dukes. I'm sure once you dug far enough, you'd find ties to the Gilmores as well, despite there being no obvious bribes."

"You said you knew who it was?"

Penelope told her.

Kitty's brow lifted in surprise, and she tilted her head in understanding. "How do you know for certain?"

"Call her and we'll find out."

"And just what am I supposed to say?"

Penelope told her word for word.

It was obvious Kitty was confused, but she smirked and picked up the phone all the same. She requested a connection to the correct residence and, unlike last time, she was put through to the exact person she was calling for.

Kitty grinned even broader at Penelope as she spoke:

"I know all about Minerva. Meet me tomorrow at ten a.m. in the Abercrombie Tea Room or you'll be reading about it in the next edition of the *New York Tattle*."

She hung up before a response could possibly be made.

"What now?" Kitty asked.

Penelope grinned. "Now, we meet with Alice Todd and hopefully nab our killer."

CHAPTER TWENTY-SIX

This time, the wait for an arrival was a far more nail-biting experience. Kitty was eager to get the perfect first nip at a story that would probably sell out that edition of the *Tattle*. Penelope just wanted justice.

They were seated in an even more secluded and strategically chosen corner of the Abercrombie Tea Room. Fortunately, it was mostly empty this time of day between the usual meal times, which was why it had been chosen.

Five minutes ticked by past the designated meet time.

"I should have known she'd be too cunning to actually—"

"She's here!" Kitty exclaimed.

Both of them stared in surprise and relief as Eleanor Winthorpe walked in and headed toward them.

"Hello, Eleanor," Penelope said in a neutral tone.

"I suppose I shouldn't be surprised to find you here as well, Penelope. I knew this was a setup."

She took the seat across from them and sat down, giving them an expectant look.

"If you're hoping I'll confess something, I'm afraid you'll have to be disappointed."

"Why did you even bother showing up?" Kitty asked.

Eleanor glared at her. "To keep you from making a huge financial and occupational mistake. As it is, if you think you'll be writing for any paper in New York after this, you're sorely mistaken. Even the ones my family doesn't own will somehow find it in their best interest to turn you away at the door. This story you *think* you have? Don't waste your time writing it. It will never see the light of day."

That threat ignited something in Penelope and she could no longer remain silent.

"I think Kitty deserves an answer as to why you manipulated her. Frankly, I'd like one myself."

Eleanor shifted her attention to Penelope, the same cool, aloof look back in place. "Whatever do you mean, Penelope?"

Pen had come expecting resistance and denial and wasn't dissuaded by Eleanor's pretense of ignorance.

"Allow me to walk you through the steps that got me to the truth—and got you here as well, despite your protests."

Eleanor simply smiled, but there was an icy tint to it.

"It was the pearls that ignited the first spark, specifically those once owned by Alice Todd. I had a talk with her earlier this week. She mentioned two things that I didn't take note of at the time, though I should have. Granted, they didn't seem all that relevant back then.

"We all know that Constance liked to take things that belonged to others. And when I say take, I mean fully, as in making sure the other person no longer has any use for it."

If Eleanor was catching on, she didn't show it.

"Usually, that was by means of a threat, as she used

with Alice. You see, Alice had stopped wearing her pearl earrings, the ones that matched the pearl necklace Constance had on that day of the luncheon. The same was true of Marie, she had stopped wearing pink when she knew she'd be seeing Constance. Alice said the same thing about you and a certain scarf—the very one John had given you. The same one he no doubt bought for Constance, either that or she bought herself, hoping you might think he'd bought it for her. Either way, she taunted you with it enough to keep you from wearing it."

Eleanor had a well-practiced facade of stoicism, but Pen saw the barest hint of a twitch in her right eye.

"However, on the day of the luncheon, Alice wore her pearl earrings. Do you know why? For her, it was an act of defiance. She intended to stand up to Constance that day, and wearing those pearl earrings sent a message. Whatever hold she had over her was gone."

"You were wearing your scarf that day!" Kitty accused, unable to help herself. "I hadn't seen you wear that thing in a year."

Now, there was a slight narrowing of the eyes.

"I think we know what message you were sending, Eleanor," Pen said.

"Do you?" she replied in a bored tone.

"When combined with everything else it's not difficult to surmise. Tell me, was the message for John or Constance? Perhaps both of them. You couldn't stop yourself from flaunting your final act of revenge, because, despite everything else, this was also vengeance on your part."

"As you stated, you've certainly *surmised* quite a bit, but you have yet to *confirm* anything," Eleanor replied with a satisfied smile.

"You're right," Penelope said. "But you were one of the first people in the dining room. That gave you the perfect opportunity to put the poison in Constance's glass. Then, the next evening you came to see me, which at first I thought was a convenience as it saved me the trouble of finding a way to question you. I should have known that was a bit *too* convenient, but you did provide a good excuse; you wanted to save me the trouble of supposedly embarrassing you."

Eleanor yawned as though she was thoroughly bored.

"The problem is, Eleanor, you didn't *have* to tell me a thing. Constance was dead, and she was the only one who *supposedly* knew your secret. There was no reason I had to know exactly what that secret was. It would have made more sense for you to simply state there was one, and leave it at that. The only reason Marie and Alice confessed theirs is because they no longer had a reason to keep their secrets to themselves."

Penelope laughed softly and tilted her head to consider Eleanor, whose facade of boredom looked slightly more sullen.

"Once again, you couldn't help yourself, could you? I do have to say, you certainly are a master manipulator. Constance could have learned something from you on how to do it right. You had me completely enthralled with your ideas about becoming an independent woman, and living a life of adventure, defying societal expectations. You probably knew your audience well enough. But not all that well..."

The bored look was gone and Eleanor stared at Penelope with a steady gaze.

"You know that strange ability I have of recalling everything? Well, I know exactly which books are located where in the library Agnes left to me. Second bookcase on the south wall, fourth row from the bottom, eighth book from the left. The exact one you stopped in front of before turning to me and revealing your supposed secret."

A small, ironic smile curled one side of Eleanor's lips, but she didn't respond.

"That would be *Tess of the d'Urbervilles*. A story that begins when the heroine falls asleep and crashes the family cart, killing the horse that was the only source of their livelihood. It's a tragic tale from that point on, enough to tug at anyone's heartstrings. Also oddly similar to your tale of the chauffeur.

"Then of course there's the far more exciting tale of traveling the world in eighty days by Jules Verne. The very book that was on the shelf just past my shoulder as you went on to thrill me with your ideas of living a life that defied societal expectations. Every precocious young girl was fascinated by Nellie Bly and her independent trip around the world in less than eighty days. Most probably aren't as familiar with Amelia Earhart, but any young lady who lives her life reading the adventures of others probably would be."

Eleanor still couldn't keep the slight smile from her face, no doubt enjoying how well she had tricked Penelope.

"Which was another thing that struck me as odd. When I questioned John, being that you conveniently shifted the suspicion to him, he told me you were never interested in doing that sort of thing, not in real life. Sailing, racing cars, I doubt you even got your New York pilot's license. It was all just a ruse to distract me, wasn't it? To win over my sympathies and endear me to a like-minded woman.

"Then, there was that second thing Alice told me just before we parted ways. She mentioned that Detective Beaks already considered me a prime suspect by the time he got to her, 'what with my experience and all.' I thought she was referring to what I'd experienced at the hands of Constance and Clifford. You even confessed yourself that you told him that much, which was likely to come up with any of the others he talked to. But then you claimed you never told him about my prior case involving poison. I had to have another chat with Alice yesterday to confirm that was what she had meant by experience, it was my experience at handling a case involving poison."

"You tricked me too!" Kitty accused. "*You're* the one who told me I should pester John for the cigarette case earlier this year. I don't even smoke, well, not that much. I'll bet you're also the one who told Constance I had one just like hers."

Penelope leaned in and gave Eleanor a penetrating look. "You see, it's all these little lies and manipulations, Eleanor. You can't keep from doing it, and now it's gotten you into trouble."

Eleanor stared at them for a long, dramatic moment. Then she laughed, slowly clapping her hands.

"Oh you two, you should see the looks on your faces. I wish I could frame it. Don't be too offended. Most people don't catch on to what I'm doing. At least with you, Pen, I had to be inventive. I know so many women like you. So aching to be free and *modern* you get stupid over it."

"So you're admitting it?" Penelope asked in surprise, not even caring about the insult.

"Admitting what? That you two were the most gullible people I've met so far? Sure, why not?" She said with a shrug. She reached into her purse and pulled out a cigarette case, this one in black and gold. As she put a cigarette in her mouth and lit it, she lifted the case and winked at Kitty. "This is a new one I bought for myself. I knew Benny of all people would put my old one to good use somehow, either with you or Constance."

"Constance didn't even care," Kitty said. "In fact, she had the nerve to laugh at me about it."

Eleanor arched an eyebrow as she pulled the cigarette away and breathed out a sigh of smoke. "Yes, I suppose that backfired."

"You did all this just to get back at John for leaving you for Constance?" Kitty asked.

"No, she did it for money," Penelope said, eyes on Eleanor.

"Do tell, Penelope," Eleanor said, eyes wide with interest. "This should be good."

"I think after you saw John kiss Constance and you decided you were done with him, you devised a plan to at least make money from it, all while exacting your revenge. You pushed him toward her, knowing what that match would do for the stock price of the Duke family's holdings. Once the marriage was announced, the stock price went up as expected. You even cemented things by making sure Constance became chair of the Young Ladies Historical Preservation Society. I'm guessing you were the one vote that gave her the win. Saving the Duke House would be an obvious project. John probably even told you about his concerns regarding Frederick Carpenter and Park Avenue First while you were still together.

"Considering everything else you were able to dig up on others, I'm sure you knew about Constance and Salvatore.

You sent Mabel information that she forwarded to Salvatore to pass on to Constance; information she could use to bully and blackmail people into voting for her, because really who would actually *want* to vote for Constance? With your connections in media, you could easily find dirt on fellow members. When she won, and poorly kept rumors about which house she was preserving spread, the share price in their stock went even higher.

"But that wasn't enough, not with the tiny bit you'd been given when you turned twenty-one. I'm guessing for the average person it would have been a fortune, but for a Winthorpe, not so much."

"I do hope you're getting to some point that makes sense because right now it doesn't," Eleanor said after exhaling again.

"True, there probably isn't much money to be made in a match that everyone knows about. Even the bump they got when they moved the wedding date up, well ahead of the election. But there *is* money to be made if there is a surprise that upsets all of those plans."

"Like murder," Kitty finished for her.

"Which is where Minerva comes in," Penelope said.

"Roman goddess of war, yes? Whatever does that have to do with me?" Eleanor asked innocently.

"It took me a moment to make it fit with everything else, but then it all made sense, in part because of you. Constance and John kissing, in your home, on your birthday—a moment that should have been in your honor. That's how you put it, yes? Just like the goddess of war finding Medusa and Neptune in the temple built to honor her. It was the woman that paid the ultimate price there too."

Kitty laughed. "You *were* jealous after all!"

"Shut up, Kitty," Eleanor spat in anger.

Penelope realized they had finally pierced her armor of indifference. Eleanor was good at maintaining a facade, but her jealousy was something she couldn't contain. Pen pressed on.

"Despite all your protestations about not wanting to be married, you were still seething inside about what John and Constance had done, weren't you? At first, I think all you wanted to do was humiliate her the way she had done with you. You were the one to suggest Kitty pester John for the cigarette case, and yes, as Kitty suggested, you did in fact slip that bit of information to Constance hoping that she would call off the wedding at the last moment."

Pen thought back to Constance and Salvatore in the courtyard. Knowing everything she knew now, she was almost certain Constance had known she and Kitty were watching her as she pulled out the cigarette case and then flaunted her engagement ring.

"I suppose that's when you learned that Constance and John had an arrangement with each other. Neither cared if the other cheated, they certainly weren't going to ruin the lucrative plans for their nuptials over it. Unfortunately, by then you had already borrowed the stock to short via the corporation you'd set up, Minerva. When the price failed to go down, you became desperate. You mailed Kitty the information about corruption and bribes, hoping the story would come out and cause a dip in the price."

Kitty breathed out a laugh that was slightly disgruntled.

"What you hadn't counted on was that Kitty would tell John. At the time, she had no idea that further digging would lead a trail right back to the Dukes. They quickly scrambled to squash the story before it could be published, thus ruining your plans once again."

Eleanor was now visibly tense, no doubt reliving the

panic that must have set when her second attempt to short the stock had failed.

"By now the investment company was probably calling in the loan, which meant resorting to more drastic means. You sent the letter to Mabel instructing her to make sure the punch was served at the tables ahead of time. But then John called you and said he was going to be there. That might be problematic as your history with him and Constance would no doubt point the finger at you. You could put on a show of being indifferent to the breakup and the subsequent engagement, but rumors do have a way of festering. You'd heard the mutterings and saw the surreptitious glances."

Eleanor was breathing heavier now, on the verge of snapping.

"It would definitely cast suspicion on you, so you thought of a way to allay it. You had your aunt invite me. After all, my breakup wasn't quite so amicable, and this was the first time I'd seen Constance in ages. In fact, my very presence at the luncheon would be suspicious since I wasn't even a member. What better motives for murder than jealousy and resentment? You know a thing or two about that, don't you Eleanor? It was all the more satisfactory after working so hard to build Constance up and bolster the Dukes' companies. It would have made the fall that much more enjoyable. When it first backfired, it was a slap in the face wasn't it?"

Eleanor was seething inside, Penelope could tell, even through that rapidly cracking stoic demeanor.

"Do you know what your mistake was?"

Eleanor was too incensed to reply, even in the mocking tone she'd used up to now. She stabbed her cigarette into the ashtray.

"The stamps."

Her eyelashes fluttered in surprise.

"I couldn't figure out why you'd used different stamps for the later letters. At first, I thought maybe two different people had sent them, but everything else was identical. And you were meticulous, for the most part. The stationery was nice but commonplace. The lettering was nothing that could be tied to your own handwriting. You even used gloves so there were no fingerprints.

"Except...you ran out of stamps sometime last year after you'd sent the first set of letters to Mabel. Those were 2-cent stamps, which is the current cost to send a letter. When it came time to send a letter to Kitty, you were desperate. Same for the letter you sent to Mabel. No time to go out and buy a new page of stamps, so why not use the ones already lying around in your home?

"The last time 3-cent stamps were used was during the Great War when they raised the cost to send a letter by one cent. In fact, when it ended they issued a special stamp in 1919 the 3-cent Victory Issue stamp. When the government lowered the price back down to 2 cents, your household probably bought a new page of stamps, not wanting to use up those special stamps. Six years, that's at least how long those 3-cent stamps have been sitting there after their initial use. Six years to be pushed around, set aside, moved, picked up, put down. Six years to collect fingerprints, both yours and those of the people who live with you."

The color drained from Eleanor's face.

"Do you remember how much you admired the René Gauthier art nouveau, stained glass window in my library? I suppose you don't remember leaving prints on it with your left hand? The same hand one would use six years ago if they were holding onto a sheet of stamps to tear off a single one for mailing. You may have used gloves in every part of your most recent scheme. If only you and your family had the foresight to use gloves six years ago. So far, everything I've said I have, as you put it, surmised." Pen leaned in closer. "But fingerprints are *confirmation*, Eleanor."

Kitty barked out a laugh. "Oh my goodness! Done in by a 3-cent stamp?"

"Shut up!" Eleanor screeched.

Penelope couldn't stop herself from pushing on.

"The one woman who had taken what was yours, humiliated you on what should have been one of the happiest days of your life, flaunted it in front of everyone, and with a wedding that was set to be *the* wedding of the season, if not the year. And now Constance still has the better of you. Your jealousy and resentment made you sloppy. It made you *stupid*. At every turn, Constance thwarted your efforts and probably laughed while doing it. Now she's got the better of you from beyond the grave. All over something as simple as a single stamp. She took everything, she *had* everything, none of which she deserved—"

"You're damn right she didn't deserve it! That conniving little witch didn't deserve a damn thing—except for murder. I only wish she *had* turned into the monster that she is, and then had her head chopped off just like Medusa. Sulfuric acid was too good for her. I'm only glad I was there to witness it."

Penelope simply stared, first in shock, then with a growing smile on her face.

"You should have maintained that stoic facade, Eleanor. I suppose you've been holding it in so long, it was bound to come out in the worst possible way, and thus, be your downfall."

"What are you talking about?" Eleanor said, in sudden confusion.

"How did you know it was sulfuric acid?" Kitty prodded.

"She *shouldn't* know that," Penelope said, still staring at Eleanor.

The realization slowly dawned on Eleanor. She had been tricked into confessing.

"The stamps...?"

"No fingerprints," Penelope said with a smile and a shrug. "You must have wiped them clean when you licked one side and then pressed down on the other with your gloved hand. The sulfuric acid on the other hand—"

"Nonsense, it's—I was told about that! It isn't as though it's difficult to get that information," Eleanor said, her breath coming in heavier.

"The police wouldn't have released that information to the general public, not even you. The only people who knew were the detectives and the innocent man they currently have in jail."

"How do *you* know it is then?" she accused.

"I am privy to a certain member of law enforcement. In fact, he's here right now."

"What?" Eleanor went completely pale, then even whiter when Detective Prescott exited the well-hidden door to the storage closet behind where they were seated. They had chosen this section of the tea room for good reason.

"You think you can arrest me? On *that* alone? My lawyers will have a field day with this. One tiny utterance that could be easily explained away? Ha!"

"I think once the police do a little digging into the Minerva company, they'll find more proof. Based on the letters you sent to Mabel—and I trust they'll easily find the sources who gave you all the information contained in them—you knew Constance and the gardener were having secret trysts. Yet another far more vulnerable person for the police to place the blame on instead of you. It was perfect...almost. I should point out, you weren't wearing gloves that day. How careful were you about touching the container that held the sulfuric acid? Did you wipe the door to the storage closet? Constance's glass?"

At this point, Eleanor was completely closed off, but Pen could see the tell-tale signs of uncertainty in her eyes.

"At any rate, Miss Winthorpe yes, right now we do have enough to arrest you on," Detective Prescott said, nodding toward the window, where two police officers had been waiting in an unrecognizable car.

"What? How dare you!" Eleanor said, spinning around in horror. She wisely went silent as they walked in and put the handcuffs on her, realizing that her mouth had already gotten her into trouble.

Her eyes did enough talking to convey her feelings. Penelope certainly wouldn't have any friends among the Winthorpes from now on. Poor Cousin Cordelia would never be invited to lunch with Mrs. Winthorpe again.

"You've certainly been keeping a lot from me," Kitty said with a pout once they had walked Eleanor out. "But I suppose this makes up for it."

"I can do you one better," Penelope said with a smile. "Alice Todd, she can fill in a lot of the blanks for you about this bribery scheme, which did in fact happen, definitely a story worthy of the *New York Times*."

Penelope rose up and turned to Detective Prescott with an even broader smile.

"Congratulations on solving yet another case, Miss Banks."

"Are we still being official?" she teased.

"I am still acting in my capacity as a detective." His eyes

softened. "And this one was personal for you. Are you alright?"

Penelope took a breath and slowly exhaled. "I am. Despite everything, I'm not happy Constance is dead. I've been over what happened between us long ago. Mostly, I'm angry at being used so horribly. I can't believe how gullible I was."

"I hate to add salt to that wound but I could have told you New York doesn't issue pilots licenses, in fact, no government agency does. It's done through a private organization, the National Aeronautics Association."

"How do you know about planes?" Her eyes darted to his scar. "Do you fly?"

His eyes lost focus for a moment. "I did, once upon a time."

Penelope gave him a penetrating look. "One of these days you're going to ask me to dinner and you're going to reveal everything about yourself, Detective Richard Prescott."

A slow grin came to his face and his lovely dark eyes refocused on her again. "One day I will, Miss Penelope Banks. Perhaps on our next case?"

"Ohh-hoo," Kitty teased. "Someone has a new beau."

They both blinked and gave her irritated looks.

"I suppose I should escort Miss Winthorpe down to the proper precinct. I'm sure there will be one young man happy to be released from jail as soon as possible."

"Indeed."

They said their goodbyes and he left.

"So, another case for the lady detective solved. That should be good for business," Kitty said, standing up.

"I don't know, I have a feeling I'll be persona non grata with a lot of influential families in this city after this one."

"Welcome to the club," Kitty grinned. "What do you say we ditch the tea room and do something illegal by getting a proper drink? We might as well be guilty of something."

"That's my kind of crime."

EPILOGUE

"I feel like I'm being manipulated yet again," Kitty groused, staring across the table at Benny.

They were having drinks later the next week at the Peacock Club: Penelope, Jane, Benny, and Kitty.

"I can't deal with discord in my life. Benny, I adore you. Kitty, I'm...definitely warming to you."

Kitty frowned. Benny grinned.

"But you two are more alike than you think. So...reconcile right now."

Benny remained stubborn, but Kitty gave him a sheepish look. "I never intended to print names in that article, Benny. My editor insisted. Why do you think I've wanted to leave for something more prestigious for so long?"

"Benny?"

He pursed his lips and narrowed his eyes at Kitty. "I suppose I can thaw just a little, but I still don't entirely trust her."

"I'm fine with that. I kind of like our spats."

An amused smirk twisted his mouth, telling Pen he liked them too. Zounds, they were impossible.

"I like your spats too! I'm learning so much from them," Jane said with an ossified giggle.

Everyone laughed. Two glasses of champagne and she was a completely different woman.

"I hope at least you've stopped canoodling with John Duke?" Pen said, giving Kitty a pointed look.

Kitty scrunched her nose with disdain. "Too much bad luck there. Every woman in his life came to a bad end. I certainly didn't want to be next. With all this business of bribery, scandalous court cases and most likely losing the trolley car lines, no one wants to do business with the Dukes. John's money won't last even one generation. Besides, like you, I have my new career to focus on with the *New York Register*, one of the few papers not owned by the Winthorpes."

"Speaking of the Winthorpes I see that they have already started their media campaign to help clear Eleanor," Benny said.

"It won't work, I have a source that says the police already tied Minerva and the short sale of the stock to her. Combined with all the proof we gave them, she'll no doubt be convicted." Penelope frowned. "But they certainly got their revenge on me."

"How so?" Benny asked with a grin.

"Nothing scandalous enough for you, though Cousin Cordelia is certainly in a state. Mrs. Winthorpe stole my maid, offered her twice the pay! I tried to warn poor Jenny, but apparently her cousin works for Mrs. Winthorpe as well and she'd like to be with her. I couldn't fault her for that."

Pen grinned and took a small sip before continuing. "But I got my revenge."

"Oh?" Kitty prodded.

"Let's just say I learned something about price manipulation from this case. I offered Jenny twice as much, knowing Mrs. Winthorpe would top that pay. I knew she was only trying to steal my maid for revenge. Sure enough, she did. I told Jenny to hold firm and make sure her cousin got the same absurd increase in pay."

"You sly devil," Kitty said with a laugh.

"I, for one, am always a fan of helping the proletariat classes whenever possible," Benny said.

"You're the last person I'd suspect of holding communist tendencies," Pen said, eyeing his fashionable clothes.

"But it seems our Alice is," Kitty said with a smile. "Now that it looks like the Todds' bank may have to close its doors, she and that construction boy-o of hers are blousing off to California. Something to do with the farmworkers out there."

"Good on her finding her own way in life," Penelope said, lifting her glass. She hoped Alice and Liam were happy. Pen had used her connections with the police—or at least her one and only connection—to retrieve all the pearls and the clasp from her grandmother's necklace, which Alice had been grateful for.

The performer of the night, Lucille "Lulu" Simmons, had just finished her set and came over to join them. Lulu was a jazz singer who had been the one to help Penelope find her footing in the world of illegal gambling back when she was on the nut.

"Was that you all talkin' through my song?" she scolded, pouring herself a glass of champagne and glaring at them. "I should be offended."

"Just burying the hatchet between these two," Penelope said, eyeing Benny and Kitty.

"I'm just disappointed I didn't get to participate in this

case of yours. Rich folks fighting, and I coulda had ringside seats?"

"And been splattered with the sweat and blood from all of it," Penelope said. "It was messy."

"Now, who doesn't love a good mess?"

"Hear, hear, sister," Benny said, lifting his glass to her. Lulu laughed and tapped her glass against his.

"You're welcome to join me if you ever want to quit your day job," Penelope hinted, not for the first time. "I could always use a smart partner."

She quickly turned to Jane, who was now zozzled up to her eyeballs from champagne and couldn't have cared less. "*Another* smart partner, I mean."

"Aww, thanks, Penelope," the ossified Jane said, for once using Pen's first name.

"Hey," Kitty said. "I could be a partner too. I'm pretty smart."

"I thought I already *was* a partner," Benny said with a pout.

"Okay, from now on, I'll include you all in my cases, are you all happy?"

"Yes," they all said, much to her surprise. Then she considered it. "I suppose you each have your, um, talents."

"Chin, chin!" Benny said, raising his glass.

There was a sudden commotion on the dance floor that drew their attention.

Penelope wasn't surprised to see Tommy Callahan, dangerously handsome, and the number one henchman for Mr. Sweeney, a notorious gangster.

She *was* surprised to see him with a very young blonde. Usually, he was the solitary type, smoking a cigarette at a table by himself as he watched the act of the night. Then again, it didn't look like these two were exactly dancing the

Texas Tommy. In fact, he was dragging the very reluctant, and very drunk woman off the floor.

"Trouble on the dance floor, it seems," Benny hummed.

"Trouble indeed," Lulu said, her cool, easy demeanor hardening with worry.

"What is it?" Penelope said, curious about that look.

Lulu quickly masked it and turned to her with a sardonic smile. "Nothing a good spanking can't handle. At any rate, tell me more about this case. I want *all* the dirt."

Before she began, Penelope's eyes shifted from Lulu to the dance floor where Tommy and the girl had suddenly disappeared. There was definitely something going on at the Peacock Club. But she was still recovering from this case, and right now it was none of her business.

The last thing she wanted to do was go looking for more trouble....

CONTINUE ON FOR YOUR FREE BOOK!

AUTHOR'S NOTE

It was quite a bit of fun researching this story. I wanted to write a book that took place on Park Avenue, one of New York City's most famous. Sometimes your research can take you down a rabbit hole of a far more interesting story. Thus, this book is loosely based on reality.

As it happens, there was a fight over extending Park Avenue from 34th to 32nd. The original 1 Park Avenue was held by a widow of a diplomat named Martha Bacon. A man named Henry Mandel did in fact buy those two blocks via a corporation named One Park Avenue Corporation. For obvious reasons he requested the extension of Park Avenue to ensure the name was accurate to the address.

There was quite a bit of back and forth between the mayor and the Board of Aldermen. It eventually went to the highest court in New York, the New York Court of Appeals, which finalized the terminus of Park Avenue at 32nd Street. Changing parts of 4th Avenue to Park Avenue South didn't come until 1959, for unrelated reasons.

As for the election, there was a lot of creative license thrown in for the story, which should not be taken as fact.

AUTHOR'S NOTE

The only nod to reality is that the mayoral candidate in this story Mickey Driver is very much based on Jimmy Walker, particularly where he stood on the issues. This includes his promise to get rid of trolley cars (which never really happened for political reasons once he was elected). He was a fun character who was known to visit speakeasies and spend a little too much time with chorus girls. Spoiler alert: he won the election.

I certainly plan on including Mickey Driver in future books with a more prominent role. How could I not?

Finally, yes there was a bit of tongue-in-cheek fun with the last names—five in total throughout the book. If you catch the reference, I hope you at least got a chuckle out of it. (Hint: google the names from chapter one, if you're still clueless)

CONTINUE ON FOR YOUR FREE BOOK!

GET YOUR FREE BOOK!

Mischief at The Peacock Club

**A bold theft at the infamous Peacock Club.
Can Penelope solve it to save her own neck?**

1924 New York
Penelope "Pen" Banks has spent the past two years making ends meet by playing cards. It's another Saturday night at The Peacock Club, one of her favorite haunts, and she has

GET YOUR FREE BOOK!

her sights set on a big fish, who just happens to be the special guest of the infamous Jack Sweeney.

After inducing Rupert Cartland, into a game of cards, Pen thinks it just might be her lucky night. Unfortunately, before the night ends, Rupert has been robbed—his diamond cuff links, ruby pinky ring, gold watch, and wallet...all gone!

With The Peacock Club's reputation on the line, Mr. Sweeney, aided by the heavy hand of his chief underling Tommy Callahan, is holding everyone captive until the culprit is found.

For the promise of a nice payoff, not to mention escaping the club in one piece, Penelope Banks is willing to put her unique mind to work to find out just who stole the goods.

This is a prequel novella to the *Penelope Banks Murder Mysteries* series, taking place at The Peacock Club before Penelope Banks became a private investigator.

Access your book at the link below:
https://dl.bookfunnel.com/4sv9fir4h3

ALSO BY COLETTE CLARK

PENELOPE BANKS MURDER MYSTERIES

A Murder in Long Island

The Missing White Lady

Pearls, Poison & Park Avenue

Murder in the Gardens

A Murder in Washington Square

The Great Gaston Murder

A Murder After Death

A Murder on 34th Street

Spotting A Case of Murder

The Girls and the Golden Egg

Murder on the Atlantic

LISETTE DARLING GOLDEN AGE MYSTERIES

A Sparkling Case of Murder

A Murder on Sunset Boulevard

A Murder Without Motive

ABOUT THE AUTHOR

Colette Clark lives in New York and has always enjoyed learning more about the history of her amazing city. She decided to combine that curiosity and love of learning with her addiction to reading and watching mysteries. Her first series, **Penelope Banks Murder Mysteries** is the result of those passions. When she's not writing she can be found doing Sudoku puzzles, drawing, eating tacos, visiting museums dedicated to unusual/weird/wacky things, and, of course, reading mysteries by other great authors.

Join my Newsletter to receive news about New Releases and Sales!
https://dashboard.mailerlite.com/forms/148684/72678356487767318/share

Printed in Great Britain
by Amazon